AMANDA'S COVE

A Maine Coastal Tale

Roy P. Fairfield

Bastille Books
Saco, Maine

Bastille Books ™
P.O. Box 1648
Saco, Maine

Library of Congress Catalogue Card Number: 89-90811

ISBN: 0-9621921-1-2

Cover Design by Dan Howard
Graphic JAM

To:

Steve Rumery,

who stimulated my
imagination with big
questions about tiny
scraps of evidence...

Table of Contents

Chapter I

The Discovery

Amanda had been missing three days that morning he decided to rummage the beach before going to work. Waves were still dashing high on the rocks following a week of heavy seas, and he noted that combers were still breaking loud and white across the mouth of the cove. Seaweed and sand churned with each wave, and the windrow of debris against the cobbles lying against the dunes made him wonder.

Strolling slowly he walked along the sand, musing over his boss's questions during those three days. Where was Amanda? Had she ever left him before? Could she swim? Had she strayed too close to the rocky point and been swept overboard? What did he think?

Groggy from lack of sleep, he reviewed his answers. She had never left him before. He was as puzzled as Mr. Curtis seemed to be. She could swim but what chance did she have in that boiling sea all week? He knew he did not dare to think or say too much. In the five years he'd worked on Boss Curtis's farm, he'd not been given much chance to say what he thought. The one time he expressed an opinion about the farmer's horse, he'd been told in blunt terms, "Look, you black-assed nigger, you're lucky to be here. You take orders and you don't tell me nothin'!"

As he approached the end of the beach and heard one of Curtis's roosters crow and watched the sun trace a path through heavy mackerel skies, he knew rain would come before the day was out. He'd hardly noted that in his mind, dazed for lack of sleep, when he suddenly spied what looked like a human arm in the seaweed. It shocked him almost into insensibility...and he half ran and half walked toward a pile of weeds that had swirled around the back of a huge boulder on the beach. He felt the pull to run away, but he knew he couldn't. The arm was like a magnet.

Finally he stood over the pile, nearly fainting when he saw that the arm was black. Could it be? Suddenly he dropped to his knees and began pawing at the seaweed as a dog might. Quickly he knew what he'd found, his pulses and heart moving so fast, he thought his chest would break. First the whole arm, then the chest...Amanda's breasts! Then the rest of her torso!

In seconds he was in tears, fell over her dead body, sobbing sobs that wracked him from head to toe. And she did not move, so he knew...

Equally as quickly he got scared, for he saw bruises the sea had not washed away. Could it be that she was murdered or died in a fight? Or was she thrown overboard by somebody stronger that she? All these questions rushed through his mind in torrents.

Dan knew he might be in trouble if anybody saw him lying in a pile of seaweed so he looked around slowly and carefully. Flight on the underground railroad had taught him to be cautious and to be prepared to flee from such troubles. Nobody was in sight although he did see a horse grazing on Hill's Neck peninsular, and the rooster still crowed from the farm. Gulls, too, were pecking through the piles of debris on the other end of the beach.

Damping his fear a bit, he coolly covered Amanda's naked body and calculated that the water would probably not reach that high on the afternoon tide...but might just before dawn the next morning. So with awakened senses, he made a plan. He would sneak down to the beach in the darkness the next morning and carry Amanda's body back to their shack before anybody could find it there in the debris.

Standing up slowly and cautiously and making each muscle move as he wanted it, he continued toward Hill's Neck as he had so many mornings before. Reaching his closest neighbor's horse, he quietly edged to the mare's head, scratched her as was his custom, then slowly ambled back along the beach where he quietly noted that neither Amanda's arm nor body was in sight. Tears almost blinded him, but he continued to the end of the grey sand, waded somewhat noisily up the rocky bank, picked up the path that passed the spring, cut back on the old King's Highway, and eventually reached the wagon road leading to Curtis's Farm.

When he got to the barn for his morning orders, there was Curtis coming through the inner shed, tucking in his shirt and fastening his overalls.

Musta just had a shit, Dan thought as the middle aged farmer said "Mornin'" and picked up a pitch fork.

"Heard anything from Amanda, Dan?" Curtis asked, almost softly.

"No suh, not a thing," Dan said as calmly as he could though his heart was racing rapidly. Dan, too, picked up a hay fork, for he knew they had haying to do as

soon as the sun came through. Rain could ruin the July
hay if they didn't work hard.

Curtis said no more. Both of them knew what they
had to do, feed the hens, lay new hay for the cows, harness
the horse, hitch him to the mowing machine. So they
went about their chores, silently.

Dan was glad for that because he was too upset to
talk. But he didn't want Curtis to know that or it might
upset his plan. The two men had worked together,
sometimes elbow to elbow, ever since Dan and Amanda
arrived from Virginia five years before. Dan knew he
owed Curtis much for having given him a place to live
when the "bounty hunters" were chasing him. True his
home was a shack but he and Amanda had survived,
which was better than some of his fellow and sister
railroad riders had done when hounds and shotguns
found their prey. Also, since the Civil War had broken
out only a few seasons after they arrived and Mr. Curtis
had promised them five acres of land and their freedom,
he knew he had to be careful or risk losing it. Yet he
couldn't quite shake from his mind the possibility that
Amanda might have met foul play at the Curtis house
three nights before. After all, she had gone there late in
the afternoon to help with supper. Also, she was
beautiful and sexually alluring despite years of hard labor
in the tobacco fields and at least one whipping by her
white master in Virginia. But Dan tried to root these
thoughts from his mind as he did his chores routinely.

And thus the day passed, routinely, although Dan
was fearful that Curtis might have suspected something
was wrong when they drove the haywagon across the
beach and Curtis caught him looking out to sea.

"What's the matter, Dan, seen somethin'?"

Dan turned back to his owner and calmly replied, "Nope."

"But you're awful quiet today."

"Just thinkin' 'bout powah of them combers," Dan remarked, as casually as possible.

"Yeah," Curtis responded, "wouldn't want ta be in 'em today."

That was his only scare. They cut hay, waited for it to dry, turned it over with their forks, and pitched it onto the wagon...in time to beat the thunder shower that roared in over the southwest corner of the marsh at mid-afternoon. They pulled the hay wagon into the barn, and Curtis observed that he was tired because he hadn't slept well. "Ate too much, I guess," he remarked, cryptically. Uncharacteristically, he added, "Let's call it quits, pitch it off tomorrow. As soon as the rain lets up, why don't you go home and see if Amanda is there? Sure do miss her around here."

"Yas suh, Mr. Curtis," Dan enjoined.

And as soon as the storm passed, he sauntered slowly back to his shack, knowing that it would be as empty as his hopes. Another night of loneliness, he thought, wondering how he would get his burden home without being discovered or blamed for Amanda's death.

Chapter II

The Waiting

He puttered about, frying some pork and cornmeal, but he wasn't hungry despite the hard day's work. The air was sultry since the sun was now out and steam practically rose from the marsh. He was surprised at himself, for every little movement of the oak trees overhead suggested Amanda's footsteps and he halfway expected her to burst through the rickety old door with her usual energy and smiling greetings. But as the corn and pork sizzled in the pan, he occasionally pinched himself knowing that it was not to be. When at dusk he strolled half-heartedly down the hill to fetch water from the well, he saw a doe with her fawn slipping along the edge of the marsh under the thin sliver of a first quarter moon. How he longed for Amanda back, for they always enjoyed hugging, kissing and making love under the newly rising moon. And how many times had they laughed about the position of the moon, using their inherited folklore to guide them.

"It'll be wet, Dan," Amanda would laugh. "See, it's hanging straight down and can't hold water." He could hear her voice now, even as he dipped water into the old copper kettle he had salvaged from the farm dump when Curtis threw it away. He splashed water on his face to keep him alert, and thanked his God for the cooling evening.

Climbing back up the hill to his house, he began to sweat as he wondered what he would do with Amanda's body. Should he tell Mr. Curtis and have Curtis call in the sheriff and risk living in jail the rest of his life? Would anybody believe his story? Should he bury her under the pile of rocks he'd thrown out of his garden to improve the soil? Should he borrow a neighbor's skiff and ferry her out past the cove mouth on a calm night, dump her overboard in a burlap bag with rocks to sink her to the bottom? What to do? As he considered each way of "doing it," he shuddered a bit. How could he do such a thing to the wife he had loved for ten years? with whom he had both suffered and enjoyed so much?

As he rocked in his old rocking chair, he dozed a bit and dreamed of their life together on the plantation, how they sang with their other darky friends in the twilight and around the slave house fires. He saw Amanda in all her beauty, fire flickering on her lovely brown face and in her bright eyes, and dreamed that he had asked for her that first night he ever saw her. But his dreams were shattered when the wind rose in the oaks and a small limb clattered down on his roof. It scared him for a moment until he could figure out what happened, and he stepped out on his crudely but sturdily built front porch. He saw that the moon had set in the west and Venus was glowing brightly in the last twilight's glow. So he knew in an instant that he had dozed for no more than a couple of hours. He still had time...

"Lucky for good weather," he thought as he began planning for his trip to the beach and wondered if he were strong enough to carry her back. But since he had several hours to wait, he sat down again in his chair and began to rock, humming to himself some of the spirituals he had known since he was a child..."Over Jordan," "Swing Low," "Steal Away to Jesus" and all the rest. It comforted him, and he knew that he needed to be calm to accomplish his mission. But he was tired, and again slipped into a doze and found himself escaping Virginia with a veteran of the railroad who promised to get him

and Amanda to a land where they would be free. Again,
he could see Amanda's beautiful face against his own as
they lay silent in a deep forest many miles from their
Virginian home and listened to hound dogs baying
frantically when they seemed to close in on their
prey...but lost the scent in water at the edge of the swamp.
And in his reverie, half awake and half asleep, he
remembered crossing a river in a boat between what
somebody later described as the border between Maine
and New Hampshire. These names meant nothing to
him or Amanda, but somehow they both felt freer upon
crossing that river and walking hand-in-hand along the
Maine beaches and the King's Highway until they
reached Biddeford. Luckily they met no hostile people or
dogs, but they were careful to move at night. Luckily, too,
the tide was low as they approached their appointed
destination...so they crossed the river that the natives
called "Little," wading through the shallow water. All
their possessions and clothes on their backs.

Chapter III

Moving the Body

The wind picked up at midnight and again stirred him from his reverie and he stared through the dim light at the old clock Curtis gave him and taught him to use so that he would be at work on time. It was nearly one, so he told himself that he could doze no more. He splashed some water on his face, fetched himself a cup of water, returned to his chair, then tried to review his plan. He had to get to the beach through the underbrush quietly, cross quickly over the mounds of rocky shingles on the shore, and walk along the beach to Amanda's resting place. He heard the waves pounding the beach earlier in the night so he hoped this would cover any sound he might make. But he almost gagged when he thought of having to dig her from under the seaweed and prayed he could find the spot easily without wasting much time. These thoughts brought him to tears again, but he saw no choice but to go through with his plan.

Feeling fully rested and very alert, he stepped through the door of their shack, took a quick backward glance to see that the room was in order, relieved himself at a nearby bush, then stole along the well-worn if bushy path to the beach. Through the oak and maple leaves overhead, he could see that the stars were somewhat hazy but the North Star shone bright and clear just above the Big Dipper. That was a good omen, he thought; it had guided them from Virginia to Biddeford, and he trusted that feeling even as he worried about a chance encounter with a skunk or some stranger skulking in the neighborhood. After all, he still did not know what had happened to Amanda, nor if she had met foul play.

All went well until he reached the top of the beach where he slipped on the loose shingles, set up a rock rumble and tumbled a few feet. "What would happen?" he mused, "if this happened when he had Amanda's body over his shoulder?"   But there was no turning back though shivers ran up his back when he heard Smith's dog bark down the westerly wind. "Better the wind blow that way," he thought, "than the other. At least he'll not be able to smell me."

He slipped through the darkness as a fish might slip through water, black on black on black. Only the stars and his sure-footed familiarity with the terrain guided him. He was glad that the moon had long since set even though he thought it might have been a good companion under other circumstances.

Finally, his foot hit the rock outcrop a few feet above the ebbing tide, so he knew he was close to the pile of debris which covered Amanda. Again, he fell to his hands and knees and began pawing in the seaweed. It was slimy and tough on his hands. He hit a mussel shell attached to a piece of kelp and cut himself, but he dug on. After digging a few minutes and not coming upon Amanda, he became a bit frantic...fearing that the tide or some nosey neighbor might have taken her away from him. But that worry only intensified his digging and in a matter of moments he touched her short-cropped hair. This, too, stopped him, for it brought him sharply against his worst fears and superstitions...even touching a dead body. Though he felt his heart beat as though his chest would burst, he began to run his hands along her familiar body, slipping the seaweed away from her breasts, her stomach, her thighs, her legs and feet, also straightening her out on her back as best he could.

For ever so brief a moment he forgot she was dead and reminisced about their sex life together, its beauty, its raw edges, its frustrations, its not producing the babies their slave master had wanted, its part in their rush from Virginia and up the underground trail. But the fact that she was now cold and stiff brought him to his senses, the better to do what he had to do.

Still keenly aware of the cove, the ebbing tide, the overhead planets and Big Dipper, he took a few deep breaths and prepared to leave for his shack. He stood for a moment. Listened. Smelled the salt air, even tasted the spray's heavy salt. Some kind of night bird scared him for an instant. And he heard Smith's dog again, barking at a coon, a deer or something across the marsh. He knew the dog would not cross the full river channel at night so put that worry aside.

With a deep sigh, he reached down to pick up Amanda, only to discover that he could hardly budge her. He knew, however, that she weighed no more than bags of grain he had unloaded from Curtis's wagon when he returned from town. So why couldn't he lift her although she and he were about the same build? Again, he got down low where he knew he could use his knees for leverage, but she wouldn't move. He had not calculated that she might be water soaked...or so he thought. It was not long before he realized that her legs were wedged between a huge log and the bedrock. Again, he was reluctant to touch her thighs, for they were almost sacred in his mind. But finally he pried her loose and tried again to lift her. This time he budged her into a sitting position, got even lower on her torso and tried to sling her over his shoulder. Her skin was so covered with slime that she kept slipping off. So he took off his shirt and wiped her as dry as he could before trying again to put her on his shoulder. This time she stuck, and he gradually raised himself to his feet, thanking his lucky stars there was no early morning moon and that they were still black on black on black.

But by this time he was breathing and puffing so hard and was so aware of the distance he had to carry his precious load that he staggered along the sand. It got a little easier when he took a few steps down the beach to follow the tide-packed sands. Barefooted as he was, however, he felt every shell and tiny stone marooned by the receding water. But he clung tightly to Amanda's soft body, much aware however, that it was cold against his bare chest and back.

Several times while staggering between her place of entombment and the "path" across the shingles, he set her down. During those brief rests he tried hard not to think about her cold body, rather remembered their good times together, their facing dangers together, and their love...even making love. When he reached the steep banking to carry her up the loose shingles, he knew that he must brace himself for the worst. She was an almost impossible burden. Could he make it? Would he wake the Curtis or Smith families by all his thrashing around on the smooth rocks?

After he'd tried to lift her to the top of the banking by sheer dint of strength and kept slipping back, he stopped a moment to think. Finally he devised a plan which might work? Roll her up the rocks, trigging her with large smooth shingles. He hated to do it, but he had to do something. After twenty minutes of struggle, he managed to roll her to the top, knowing he'd probably bruised her body the more with such rough treatment. But at last he was past his worst obstacle, picked her up, crossed the road, and slipped into the path leading to the house. He feared leaving clues, but had no choice. Both their bodies were so slippery, how could they leave clues? His greatest worry now: dawn was beginning to break, so he knew he'd been away from the house at least two or three hours. But he was grateful for the warm night and the fact that the mosquitoes wouldn't be swarming for another hour or so.

But as he stumbled along the path with his heavy load, he wondered what next? How could he hide Amanda's body until he'd devised a plan to bury her? Was he safe from visitors, though he knew that Curtis had rarely come to his shack in the past, mainly at holiday time. And Fourth of July was some days past. And what about stray animals? Were they a danger to him? And what about his tattered shirt? Could he mend it so Curtis would not suspect? All these questions flooded his tired body and mind. Yet he knew that he must push on, must hide her for the day if not longer.

He reached his house as a red sun peeped over the horizon and long rays began filtering through the leaves. He entered with Amanda on his shoulder and gently laid her limp body on the bedroom floor. When he saw her there in the dim light and realized the awful truth, he sank into a chair and sobbed uncontrollably. Again his reveries of their life together nearly got the better of him...their life on the plantation, their exhaustion following their vigorous underground leader walking through the countrysides of what somebody told him was Pennsylvania, their day-to-day loving there in their shack sort of in an island of safety, surrounded by marsh, woods and ocean.   Also a hostile people world which never permitted them to forget their blackness. All of this was better than slave life even though Curtis was a hard task master in a hard climate dealing with hard facts of farm and ocean.

He did not know how long he'd sat there catching breath and time. But he suddenly twitched, as though in a bad dream, and awakened to the need to do something quickly before reporting to the barn. He barely looked at Amanda, stretched out on the faded old braided rug they'd salvaged from Smith's rubbish heap. But quickly he decided. He opened the trap door to the space beneath the floor where they kept things cool. He would put her there, lay her against the deepest and coolest wall. There he had scooped out a pit for potatoes and apples and it was nearly empty...too, he could cover her with old boards he'd collected to make it easier to crawl around down there.

So sensing that he would soon be expected at the Curtis farm, he dragged Amanda to the trap door, slipped her through the opening, and half carried and dragged her along the dirt bottom of the cellar space. He spoke to her in whispers as though she might hear. "Come on, Amanda. Easy now. All right, this won't hurt you. We gotta get you outa sight. Easy...   I don't mean to be rough..."

The whole task might have taken five minutes but it seemed to Dan like forever, he was so frightened. But he managed to climb back up to the floor of the house, looked around for tell-tale signs of Amanda's journey, covered up the trap door with the old rug, then went to the well to wash. It promised to be a beautiful day. Cicadas had begun to sing so he knew it would be hot. A squirrel cracked nuts and chattered in the branches overhead, and he was aware that the green head flies had begun to arrive, for one bit him on the back as he leaned over the pail of water to wash. Mosquitoes were in abundance, too, but they didn't bother him too much. He guessed they didn't like his black skin as much as Curtis's white.

Back at the house he put on a different shirt and clean trousers, scurrying about to hide the clothes he'd worn all night. He also discovered that a blackberry bramble had scratched his arm. Must have been coming up the path, he thought. But it was not serious so he disregarded it, then left for the Curtis place.

****

"Gonna be a hot day," he mused again as the cicadas began hissing. He also became aware of faintness and then remembered he'd forgotten breakfast. "But this is no time for weakness," he reminded himself and brushed a deer fly away from his ear. He knew he was late and wondered what Curtis would say.

Much to his surprise as he approached the barn, he saw Curtis and a soldier come toward him. This scared him for a moment; until he saw that it was Curtis's son, limping and supporting himself with a cane, too, and not some kind of police officer.

"Hi, Dan," Curtis blurted, almost cheerily. "You know Ralph, met him 'fore he went off to war."

"Howdy, suh," Dan replied, glad for the extra person present.

"Ralph's home to recuperate, came in on the train last night."

This startled Dan a bit, for he wondered if they had somehow seen him on the beach.

"Yuh, got shot at Fort Royal a few weeks ago, been in a hospital. So he'll be around here working with us to get his strength back." This caught Dan by surprise 'cause he didn't need any more people around the farm until he got Amanda to rest.

"Good," he nodded somewhat vigorously, trying to seem enthusiastic though he didn't feel that way.

"Ralph can walk OK, so I want you and him to go down on the marsh today to stake out the grass. 'Member, those farmers will be down from the country to cut salt hay this week and we gotta be ready for 'em. You know where we usually let 'em cut, Dan, so do it right."

Curtis then looked down at Dan's arm, saw it was scratched and had been oozing blood, and said, "What cha do ta ya arm? Dan?"

"Guess I scratched it chasing a skunk last night. Couldn't sleep for the noise he made, drove him away from front of th' house. But it don't hurt none."

Curtis said nothing, turned away, leaving Dan and Ralph to their devices.

It became a long day. The marsh was dry and hot. The green heads bombarded them 'til both cursed them angrily. Yet they knew they were expected to stake out the cutting section cause Farmer Jesse was always right on time and he was due in the morning. Dan didn't say much. Neither did Ralph.

Finally Ralph broached the topic Dan didn't want to talk about. "Father tells me that Amanda has gone away?"

"Yep, looks like it," Dan replied.

"Any idea where she went?" Ralph pushed.

"Nope, 'less she went back to Virginia. There was a big black man through here last week."

"But didn't she like it here in the land of freedom?"

"Guess not. Cold hard on her winters."

"Also, didn't she lose a child?"

"Yeah, last March. Nearly bled to death. Lots o' trouble since."

"Expect her back? Father and mother could use her, you know."

"Yes suh, I know."

To Dan's relief, that ended the discussion. So he now knew more than he'd learned since Amanda disappeared. But he was still puzzled. Amanda had seemed happy all day of the night she left. Even went to the Curtis farm whistling as she walked out of the house leaving Dan to his own supper. But he caught himself going into another reverie just as Ralph screamed, "Dan, wake up! Carry the rod chain toward the river!"

"Yes, suh!" he replied and walked through the salt grass that had cut his ankles so often doing this each year.

They worked silently for the rest of the afternoon, finished the task, then trudged slowly back to the barn, tools slung over their shoulders. Only when they reached the lane running past the gardens did Ralph initiate conversation.

"Gonna be here a few weeks 'til I get healed."

"Sorry ya got hurt," Dan replied.

"Don't need your pity," Ralph snapped, defensively. We're fighting this war for you, you know!"

Dan didn't know nor wholly understand though he did hear that Mr. Lincoln might free the black folk of America. But until this happened, he knew he had to be careful...even though he was given to believe that he was already free. He knew that Curtis would not take him to town and that he could not cross Curtis no matter how much he distrusted him. Nor did he dare to try to get information from Farmer Smith or local farm hands. Ever since he arrived those years back, Curtis shut him up if he asked questions. Curtis always seemed to stand between him and the world.

Again, silence continued until they reached the barn and Curtis came out to ask about their work. Ralph described the day and Curtis, standing six foot two, listened attentively but grim-faced, thumbs hooked into pants as they stood there in the yard. Dan noticed that he kept looking from his son to him and to the mouth of the cove as the gentle waves lapped against the rocks along the shore. The sun was far down the west, but it was still unusually hot.

"All right," he commanded, with a strong authoritative voice. "I want the two of you there at six in the morning when Farmer Jesse arrives. He cut in the wrong place last summer, and I don't want him to do it again. He drives his sons and animals hard. I don't want him to bargain hard with me again, understand?"

Ralph and Dan said, "Yes!" almost in unison.

"Incidentally, I saw Smith today and he reports that Jesse and his family are camped tonight up in the grove at the head of the river so you may see their campfire or hear strange noises after dark, such as singing...or even snoring." He started to chuckle at his own joke!

This last information sent shivers up Dan's back. "More people here!" he mused. Then as he put his tools away and turned to start home, Curtis took a half step toward him and observed sharply, "You know, I'm mad with Amanda, for leaving us like this. Do you really expect her back? or has she tracked off down the underground railroad? or run off with another man?

Curtis' last remark angered Dan, but he replied simply, "I dunno, Mr. Curtis. I miss her too."

Curtis stood there, thumbs hooked under the straps holding up his pants, glared at Dan, then turned back to the house.

Dan watched him amble away, slowly, wondered what he was thinking, then began to stroll home. He felt lucky that he'd gotten through the day but wondered how he could get through the night with Amanda lying stone-cold deep in the cellar. In a way he was glad that the moon would be fulling in the days ahead. It would keep him company and make the nights seem less long.

Chapter IV

Decision Time

Hungry as he was after the hard day of sweaty work, Dan had no appetite and only picked at some left over beans. He went to the well for some fresh water, sat on the upper side of the little brook that trickled out of the well, looking at the red glow over the forest across the marsh. "Hot day tomorrow," he mused.

He began to see the bright evening star that once gave him and Amanda such excitement about approaching night. And the wind was just right to hear Farmer Smith yelling at his cows as he milked them in the twilight...even heard Smith's wife calling him to eat. And this of course reminded him of Amanda's sweet voice calling him to a meal.

Before long, too, he saw the first sharp point of light from Jesse's campfire, as Curtis had predicted, and this brought him sharply back to his task of attending to Amanda's body. He felt like cursing the whole world for the dangerous situation he was in. It even flashed through his mind that he could slip out on Bayberry Point and leap off himself and end it all. But he quickly suppressed that notion, knowing that he could not abandon Amanda that way. Then he picked up the voices from Jesse's family. Since some of the songs had a rhythm like his own spirituals, he assumed that they were religious although he'd never heard them before coming north. He remembered that the year before he meant to ask Curtis about this, but did not dare for fear that the farmer would "jump down his throat."

After washing his face in the brook again and giving way to the mosquitoes, he stood silently for a moment, looked across the marsh toward Jesse's camp fire, then turned back to the house, trudging up the hill with his pail of water.

Back at home, he slumped into his favorite chair, closed his eyes and wondered what he was going to do with Amanda's body. The very thought of her sent him into sobbing convulsions for a few moments until he caught himself. He knew that he must regain his calm or all might be lost. He knew that Curtis was an unforgiving man; and though he liked the son, he did not trust him. Surely they would tolerate nothing unusual about a black man, neither questions nor strange behavior. So he began to plot in his own mind how he would dispose of Amanda's body. He knew he could not keep her close, no matter how much he loved her and depended upon her. He had to do something that would free both of them from a cruel fate...even though he did not know what that fate might be. So he ran through his mind what he could do: dig deeper in the cellar and put her there...although he felt that he had dug about as far as he could go without hitting bedrock...carry her to the large boulders at the tip of Bayberry Point and dump her overboard when the tide was leaving...though he felt that would not work because her body would probably wash back on the beach where he had found her under the heavy log. But, he speculated, she could come ashore in some other cove, be found by somebody else, and he would be blamed for her death. Furthermore, it scared him to think of Amanda back on the bottom of the ocean with lobsters, crabs and dogfish tearing at her beautiful skin. He also ruled out burying her in the marsh though he knew he could dig deep anywhere there. Wild animals would surely get her.

Finally his mind focused on the large pile of rocks that Curtis and he had thrown off the land to make room for garden plots. The pile was chest high, several paces across. If only he could get her body under the earth, under the rocks there, she would never be found. But how to move the rocks without making lots of noise? How to do it and continue work without collapsing? Sure, he was healthy, six feet tall, strong as an ox, but maybe there were limits? What if Curtis caught him in the middle of trying to do it? What excuses could he make for trying to move the rock pile when there was much more land for the taking and more rocks to throw off that land?

"Hmmmm," he muttered, half aloud, "I'll clear more land and enlarge the pile. Curtis will like that ambition and her fate would be certain." This thought stepped up his heart beat and the speed of his chair rocking, and he rocked fast for a half hour to calm down. The night was warm so he was also sweating. He walked to the water pail, dipped a clean rag into it, and wiped his face.

Back in his chair, he began to "sweat blood" again as he thought of Amanda lying in the dirt in that cool cellar. Nor could he keep his mind from the sex they had had. Just remembering it aroused him to the point of agony and frustration. Should he let himself go? Would that dishonor her? He didn't know? Long was his training against self-abuse; yet, he was tempted. His reverie was broken by a hooting owl in the trees overhead. Luckily, for he needed a clear head to make his plans carefully. So he plotted his intentions slowly and cautiously. He could make no mistakes or else, he feared, Curtis would call in the authorities. He didn't know what that meant, 'cause he didn't know who they were. But his experience told

him to make no false moves. He'd had one of those
coming up on the underground railroad and he'd nearly
bitten off the end of his heart! No more!

He thought slowly even when rocking fast. First he
would try to see which edge of the pile he could move
back a few feet toward the center of the pile. Then he
would dig as deeply as possible and bury Amanda in a
clean cloth. He began to wonder what he could take from
her to remember her by...although some of her clothes
remained. After burying her, he would then move the
rocks back over her grave and add to them to make it
appear as though nothing had disturbed the pile. He had
heard that the Indians in Western Virginia had done
that...to keep animals away, also curious humans one
generation to the next. All of this, he knew, he must do
under the cover of night; yet, if he did it soon, he knew
that the moon could be his ally. And frightened as he had
always been of shadows moving in the moonlight,
Amanda needed him to be strong now. He knew that
once he had buried her body under the pile of rocks at
night, he could use the daylight to add any number of
rocks from the nearby fields without suspicion.

Next he had to figure out, when?

Exhausted by this time, he could tell from the
setting of the half moon that he had to go to bed or be
worthless the next day. He would put off the "when"
decision until the next night or two. Again, he was
tempted to go into the cellar to view Amanda's body, but
did not yield; rather, he went out on his porch to urinate,
stirred a skunk from the neighboring bushes, then fell
into bed and almost immediately went to sleep.

Several hours later he awoke with a start. It was black as pitch. He had had a bad dream. He was on the beach where he'd found Amanda, opposite the new barn Curtis had built for marsh hay. He'd started to climb the shingled banking when all the rocks tumbled in on top of him. Being naturally superstitious, the thought of being buried in stones sent shivers up his bare back as he sat up in bed. Was God trying to tell him something? A long time getting back to sleep, again he heard the owl seeming to call his name, Down....down.....Dow....n! It was eerie, he thought, but he regained his composure by running through his mind the measuring of the marsh, the beauty of the river on a sunny day, the mournful but comforting baying of Smith's hounds, the moonlight falling across the cove that he had already decided to call "Amanda!" Nobody in the whole world, he thought, needs to know what I call the cove. But I'll know... He ran the name through his mind several times, "Amanda's Cove... Amanda's Cove... Amanda's Cove." "It is beautiful," he thought. Then cried himself back to sleep.

Chapter V

Haying With Jesse

He awoke the next morning fairly refreshed. Despite the curious dream, he had slept soundly his body was so tired. And as he recalled the dream, he looked upon it as a good sign. Perhaps God wanted **both** Amanda and him to be buried under stones? And that was better than the way some of his plantation friends had been buried after being chewed up by hounds or drowning in their own blood after being whipped by their owners. To this day he shuddered to recall such brutal events happening before his very eyes and those of his slave friends.

He quickly ended his reverie and began to think of what he had to do today. "Being with Ralph is easier than being with Curtis," he mulled. "Maybe I can get him talking about the war, that would take him off my tracks," he thought. So when they met at the barn, it was a relief that Curtis was not there. They picked up their tools, walked silently across the fields toward the river, and arrived just as Farmer Jesse drove along the old graveled road in his hayrake. Curtis was right, he was right on time.

The old farmer "from up country" greeted them gruffly, told them where he was going to cut the salt grass-hay. Ralph was quite polite with Jesse despite the running feud the farmer had with his father.

"Jesse," he remarked, quietly but firmly, "We have staked off the marsh this year. You'll cut where we tell you to cut."

This set Jesse back a pace or two. "Don't your father trust me? Where IS he anyway? And what are you doing here," failing at first to see that Ralph had part of his uniform on.

"Home from the war a piece," Ralph responded courteously. Father's busy with the animals at the barn, and I'm just helping out until my leg is fully healed.

"Didn't know ya were wounded, Ralph," Jesse responded, almost apologetically.

"I'll be all right. Let's go down to the stakes," Ralph observed, now also noting that Jesse had a couple of his sons, with shiny scythes in the back of the wagon.

So they walked together in front of the wagon down to the marsh where Dan and Ralph had worked the day before.

Jesse sputtered a bit, but softened a little. "Almanac says 'Showers this afternoon,'" he offered, seeming to want to talk.

"Yeah, guess ya gotta work fast this mornin' if ya gonna beat them," Ralph replied.

Dan rather enjoyed the conversation because it carried attention away from him. And he'd met Jesse before. The hard-hearted old farmer seemed to tolerate him, but for what reasons he didn't know. Maybe he knew something that Dan didn't know? Maybe some of his ancestors had black blood; he'd heard rumors like that.

Anyway, Dan did as he was told, walked to the river to make sure that Jesse and his sons didn't cut too close to the banking. Local myths stirred among the local population that grass close to the river contained the spirits of the early occupants of the lands, the Algonquins. Also, there was an old myth that whites would be drowned each year as a punishment for their having deliberately drowned an Indian chief's child in the river two hundred years before. Curtis believed these legends just enough to be cautious. Nor did he mind assigning Dan and Ralph the task of preserving that grass. If he needed it in an emergency, he could always cut it for himself!

Actually, it was an easy day. The wind shifted to the southwest in late morning so the ocean-cooled breezes made their lives more comfortable. The green head flies were still bad, but the two watchers cut switches from the low bushes at the edges of the marsh and occasionally brushed the pesky creatures away. Having little to do enabled Dan to review his plans for burying Amanda. Again he went over them, step by patient step so as to overlook no detail. Ralph was watching the hay makers at the other end of the staked-out grass so he did not have to worry about slipping into a conversation.

Noon also turned out to Dan's advantage. Ralph went home for lunch while he ate bread and cheese which Mom Curtis had prepared for him. So he sat a few yards from Jesse and his boys, enjoyed hearing their noisy family arguments and the glint from their sharp scythes. It gave him time, too, to wonder about Mrs. Curtis who always asked him to call her "Mom." What kind of life did she live, washing, ironing, cooking, canning vegetables and fruit? Amanda never talked too much about the woman she called "Miz Curtis," although Dan remembered occasions when Amanda would roll her beautiful black eyes into the top of her head if he speculated about Mrs. Curtis's life and what she did. But Dan never pushed her for details, figuring "Women have their secrets especially when they work for one another." But he could not remember ever having seen her sitting down except when she was doing some kind of hand work. They had the one grown son, but did she care for her ugly husband? Did they love one another? Did they ever have sex? And what might that be like? He also wondered about her body functions since he occasionally saw her flit by the window between the house and shed so figured she must be going to the back house. But he usually did not allow himself to wonder about any question all that long. There were too many things to do around the farm to waste much time wondering about things that probably were none of his business. Also Dan knew that Curtis watched him like a hawk and never let Mrs. Curtis come too close to the barn. Only once did he see her away from the house...sitting alone on a large boulder by the cove Curtis named for himself. She held a white cloth and seemed to be crying.

Since having a nap at noon was acceptable, he leaned back against one of the piles of green salt hay and closed his eyes. All he could see was rocks. And he wondered if there were as many rocks on Amanda's Beach as he had questions? What if there were a question for each rock? And what if the rocks asked their questions out loud? Would he hear both questions and answers? And through the lovely haze he heard a somewhat agitated voice, "Get up, Dan! Get up! We gotta go back to work." It was Ralph, and Dan hopped up quickly somewhat in a daze and hoping he'd not been talking in his sleep.

Nothing eventful occurred during the early afternoon. But soon the heavy black clouds began floating across the northwest. Ralph said the storm was apparently heavy over Portland, a city Dan knew about but had never visited. Thunder got so strong it rumbled the earth beneath them. Jesse and his sons scurried to load the grass and hay they had cut. Ralph and Dan pitched in to help them, even steering them toward the new barn to wait out the rain when it began to pour the proverbial bucketsful!

When the shower let up, Ralph said, "Let's go home, Dan. We can probably make your house between drops."

Dan's heart leapt into his mouth. "Ralph to my place!" he exclaimed in his own mind.

"My place isn't much," he observed.

"It's shelter and will keep us dry," Ralph observed as he led the way into the oak grove toward Dan's house.

Dan followed closely behind, racking his brain whether or not he had left anything in the open which might give Ralph any clues about Amanda. He also wondered, "Was Curtis sending him to spy?" But it was too late to do anything now because they were half way there; also, another shower was rumbling over the river to the west. But Dan's heart was pumping fast by the time they reached the little clearing in front of the house.

Ralph had taken the lead through the path and up to the front steps, but he stepped aside as they reached the door and Dan opened it to lead Ralph in. Both were rather blinded as they stepped into the dark space...made darker by the heavily clouded skies. Dan was grateful for that. "Ralph can't see much," he mused.

By this time the raindrops were pelting so heavily on the shakes of the roof that each had to shout to make the other hear.

"Kinda dark!" Ralph shouted.

"Yeah, and I forgot to get oil for the lamp," Dan replied, steering Ralph to his favorite chair. "But sit down and be comfortable." Dan moved to sit on the bed.

"Miss Amanda?" Ralph queried.

"Sumpthin' awful."

"Funny she's not back after a week."

"Yeah," Dan said, casually.

"Do you love her?"

"Yes sah?"

"Do you suspect foul play?"

Dan didn't quite know what to say, for he still didn't know how much to trust Ralph. So he replied, "Don't know? Could be she fell in the ocean? She use ta go pretty close to throw garbage over the cliff behind the barn."

Fortunately for Dan, the roof began to leak and they both laughed to hear a drip-drip-drip onto the stove.

"Gotta shingle my roof again," Dan observed.

Ralph said, "Yeah," then both men fell silent. The storm seemed to pass.

Dan was about to ask him about the war when he stood up and said, "Gotta go home or father will be wondering where I am. He would not like it, you know, if he knew I was here."

Dan stood up, but only nodded his understanding. To say anything might reveal more than he wished.

Ralph took a quick look around the cabin, fixed his gaze on the bed for a moment, then said, "See ya still got some of Amanda's clothes around," and opened the door to step out.

Dan said nothing but went to the door to see Dan leave, then watched him go down the path toward the front swamp until he went out of sight in the thick growth.

Dan returned to his chair, took a deep breath and began to review the day in his mind, hoping he had made no mistakes that would reveal what he knew about the Curtis family or Amanda.

That night he went down to what he now called Amanda's Cove to watch the moon climb out of the ocean. He wished he were a poet or could write a song about the near-round moons he had seen, pink, then red, then yellow, painting a sparkling path from horizon to shore. He had watched it rise many times, but never saw it quite like it was that night. Yet he knew that he'd always said to Amanda that the current moon was lovelier than the last. He sat on a huge boulder and stared and stared, also hearing the gentle licking of the waves on the beach. Again, he suddenly realized that he had eaten little since noon so got up and went back to his cabin to munch on bread and some blueberries he'd picked near the pathway a day or so before when coming home from the Curtis barn. He was so hungry he felt the urge to go down to the river and dig a few clams but quickly abandoned that thought for fear he might encounter an animal or stir Smith's hound dogs into a rumpus.

He passed another restless night, torn between fatigue of daily labor and thoughts of Amanda. He even tried chewing checkerberry leaves which were supposed to make you sleepy. But nothing worked. Finally, just before dawn he got up and sat in his chair and dozed...dreamed of rocks again. This time he felt his finger between two rocks, even heard them click. Woke, startled. The sun was coming up over Hill's Neck. He knew he had to get going.

The next day and the next passed fairly rapidly. The Curtis family left him alone to weed and hoe their huge garden. Also, they sent him off for a mess of clams in the river. There he was alone with the water and grass and his thoughts. It gave him time to review his plans for Amanda. He went over and over his intentions, taking each step carefully...up to the point of knowing when he would do it. Also he worried a bit about how long he could wait. How long would her body last without falling apart, especially after being in the sea at least three days? Hour after hour, Dan worked almost mechanically, hardly thinking of anything else but his life with Amanda. Over and over he ran through the beauty and the horror of their years together...loving, working in the Virginia fields, leaving their friends, trudging north through days and nights of exhaustion, loving, being pursued by hounds, arriving at Curtis' and being put in their own shack that they called "home," working through heat and cold to survive in this unfriendly climate, cooking, chopping and splitting wood, learning to fish, building and rebuilding stone walls...mostly side-by-side with Curtis since all he seemed to want was work done. He didn't care how.

Only once, on a Thursday as he later recalled, Dan was frightened. He heard a dog yelpin' "sumpthin' awful" at the barn. Then he heard Curtis swearing at the dog, "Gawd damn you, don't you ever steal pork roast again, or I'll kill you, you son of a bitch." The wind was just right to hear every word.

Dan had seen him kick the old hound before, especially when he failed to tree a coon as he should, but he had never heard him so unmercifully beat the poor creature. Dan felt every kick and spank of a board on the dog's back and secretly wished that somebody were doing that to Curtis! It all reminded him of the beatings he'd seen his fellow slaves get on the plantation. And he couldn't help but wonder about the myths he'd heard about people becoming animals when they died. Perhaps Curtis would become a dog and get his due?

His reverie was also broken on Friday when Ralph came down the row he was hoeing. Dan looked up with somewhat of a start when he heard Ralph call his name.

"Uh, howdy, sir!" he exclaimed, then wondered if his voice had given his fear away.

"Sorry I frightened you, Dan," Ralph said.

Calmer now, Dan responded, "It's all right. I wuz just payin' looks ta weeds."

Ralph proceeded to tell him that he and his mother and father would be away for the next two days. They were taking him to Portland to the hospital, would leave that afternoon and come back Sunday.

Dan's heart nearly leapt for joy, but he kept a sober face. Mr. and Mrs. Curtis had left him before. Amanda always slept in the house and he slept in the barn. He also knew what he was supposed to do to protect the farm, but he listened carefully when Ralph listed his chores.

You know what to do, Dan. Feed the animals, milk the cows, walk the boundaries Sunday morning. Check on the boat on Curtis Beach. Mom will lock the house and you are to sleep in the barn as you always do. Just keep your ear to the ground for any strangers. If anybody wants to know where we are, tell them father will be back on Sunday afternoon. I may be with them or I may not, depends upon what the doctors say about my leg.

"Are you in any pain?" Dan asked, sincerely.

Ralph responded kindly. "Not much, but I don't like the way the wound is healing. Maybe I've been doing too much here on the farm? We'll see. If I'm sent to another hospital and don't get back, I'll see you when the war is over. Rumors have it that it's going badly for our side. But President Lincoln is supposed to be working to build a stronger army."

He started to limp away as Dan said he'd do what Mr. Curtis wanted, then he turned around to say, "Incidentally, President Lincoln may issue an emancipation proclamation soon. That would be good for you, Dan."

He then turned back to the house, never giving Dan an opportunity to ask what that meant. He'd never heard such big words. But he thought to himself, "Mr. Ralph said it might be good for me. Maybe it has something to do with freedom? That's what the war's s'pose ta be about."

As he went back to his hoeing, his heart was beating rapidly. He would be on the farm, ALONE, for almost two days and all of two nights. Maybe this was the time to move Amanda? His excitement was nearly unrestrained and his heart pounding hard...until he could pull himself together and concentrate on the weeds.

A couple of hours after he had eaten the lunch Mom Curtis had prepared, he was working along side the lane leading to the barn when he heard the Curtis horse and wagon pull up to the patch he was weeding. Mr. Curtis yelled "Whoaaaa!" to the horse.

Dan looked up to see all three Curtises dressed up and the back of the wagon filled with baggage.

"Dan," Curtis exclaimed at the top of his lungs.

"Yes suh?"

"Ralph told you we were going to be gone and he told you what to do. Do you understand? ...really understand?"

Dan responded almost automatically, "Yes, suh," but thought, "It's a typical Curtis insult, but why challenge it? He'd gotten used to doing as he was told."

Mrs. Curtis spoke up. "And, Dan, I've locked the house and taken the key. But I put a package of food on

your bed in the barn. Be sure to get it before the rats do,"
she chuckled.

"Yes, maam," Dan replied, "thank you."

"You've learned your manners very well," Curtis
roared with a raucous laugh and started to whip the horse
when Ralph spoke up.

"Thank you, Dan, for showing me some of the
ropes and taking some of the load off my bad leg."

Dan was surprised by Ralph's remark, did not know
quite what to say, but lifted his arm in a kind of half salute
as a kind of thank you.

At that point Curtis turned toward Ralph, scowled a
bit then hurled one last blast at Dan, "And if Amanda
shows up, put her to work! " He then lifted the reins from
the horse's rump, tickled it with the whip, and said
"Giddy up!" The wagon rolled down the lane, leaving
Dan with his thoughts about "What next?"

Dan went back to weeding, glad for what Ralph said
and for being left alone. But he puzzled for a long time
about Curtis's instructions about Amanda. "If Curtis
knows anything about Amanda or had anything to do
with her death, why would he say what he said? Or was
this a cover-up for what he might have done to Amanda?
And why did the Curtis's lock the door when they had
never done that before? Also, they surely knew that some
of the windows were so loose they wouldn't lock. He and
Curtis had tried to make them tighter for winter, but
couldn't fix them to keep out all of the cold air. How far
did the Curtis's trust of him go? And he wondered if he

should poke about to see if he could find any clues that Amanda might have left on that fatal night?"

As he muddled his way through these questions, it suddenly occurred to him, "I must check the boat tonight to see if Curtis secured it." He often thought it strange that Curtis taught him to fish in the coves but never let him handle the boat. "Was he afraid that I might escape?"

He also knew that he had to be alert to every whisper of the evening breeze, must carry out his plan so well that he could make no mistakes. So when the afternoon had worn pretty thin, he stopped his hoeing, took his tools to the barn, then ran as fast as he could to the beach.

Sure enough Curtis had secured the boat high above the water, then tied it in a way, Dan detected, that would enable him to tell whether or not Dan had used it. This tended to confirm Dan's knowing he was not wholly trusted so he did not linger on the cobbles in which the boat was partially buried. He immediately broke into a dog trot and headed home.

"Since the full moon is due tonight," he mused, "now is the time to act."

Chapter VI

The Burial

He knew right where he would start, for he had walked round and around that pile of rocks a dozen times to determine where the rock pile was thinnest in the direction of fields and trees which needed further clearing. He had also saved some old grain bags to wrap around his hands so he could handle the rocks without tearing his flesh. Hard as his hands were, he knew that the rocks were sharp.

So he began with a vengeance while he could still see clearly, yet carefully piling the rocks in such a way that he could pull them back onto Amanda's grave without leaving room for suspicion. He worked feverishly, despite heat and mosquitoes, until early twilight. He thought the marsh was especially beautiful that evening. Still green, river rising, clouds pink and yellow with some silver tinting...all reflected in the advancing tide. Again despite the sweat and pain he was suffering, he wished that he could put his feelings into words as his people did when they sang around their campfires in Virginia...or could tumble out poems as his old friend, the Ancient Rufus, did on those hot nights when they could almost smell the cotton and tobacco growing.

He watched somewhat wistfully as the last gulls flew home to the east.

When the evening star began to shine, he knew he had to stop, go to the well to clean up, have a bite of Mom Curtis's corn bread and the last of the pork from last fall's

pig. He would then go to the barn to make certain that all
was secure for the night. He did this, however, knowing
he had plenty of time to return, for the full moon would
provide plenty of light to do what he had to do...bury
Amanda.

So back to the barn he went. Fairly fresh breezes
were blowing from Timber Island across Curtis Cove. He
always loved that fresh smell of pine and fir which came
with breezes blowing that way. But he knew he had little
time to doddle so went right to work attending to the
evening chores, tending the five cows, feeding the
chickens and pigs and bedding down the other horse. He
had done these things so many times he could do it with
his eyes closed. Yet, he knew he had to pay close
attention. "No mistakes!" he mused.

A couple of times he looked through the barn door
toward the house and it set him to wondering, again,
about the Curtises locking the place. "Didn't they trust
him?" What IF Amanda had returned, what had they
expected her to do since most of her assigned work was in
the house? It didn't make sense. Yet they also knew that
Amanda had worked outdoors, shoulder-to- shoulder
with him. Maybe that's what they had in mind? He did
know that he couldn't let his own mind drift too much
with all that he had to do before dawn. He was careful
that Rex, the old hound, was in his pen beside the barn.
He was a good watch dog and Dan might need him before
the moon went down...simply to warn him if there was
anybody around. As he fed the dog, he noted how badly
he was limping. "Curtis must have hurt him, bad!" Dan
thought, remembering his ki-yi-ing and howling as Curtis
abused him the day before.

It wasn't long before he saw the moon come up out of the ocean, a clear and huge round orange ball, at one point seeming to rest right on the ocean, but shedding no light. Dan always wondered about that, why was the moon so dark when it first appeared? Why did it take so many minutes before it sent light from horizon to shore? He even asked Curtis about it, but did not ask again when he did not understand the farmer's answer.

Again, Dan caught himself day-dreaming but soon rushed off down the lane toward his house...a trip he'd taken so many times in the five years he'd been there that he could walk or run it in his sleep. As he ran along the lane and then the path up the hill to his cabin, he looked up into the velvety moonlit sky and saw several bats diving and weaving. Was that a good omen? or bad? He didn't know. But later on he expected to have owls and whippoorwills overhead to keep him company for his awesome job. He noted, too, that the breezes had ceased and he could hear Farmer Smith across the marsh and river yelling at his dogs and wife. This at once scared and comforted Dan. He'd heard Smith so many times, it was part of the neighborhood sounds...in a rather lonesome and lonely part of the world. Yet, he hoped that Smith, sometimes a drunk, would not come ranting and raving on that particular night.

Back at his chair he decided to rest a few minutes before he started digging. Also, it suddenly occurred to him that he'd better put the pile of fresh dirt that he dug out on the subsoil under the carpet of leaves. Gosh, he thought, I almost forgot to do that. He also wondered if he'd forgotten anything else. He allowed himself to doze a little, for he knew that that would give him strength.

A few moments later, he awoke with a start. He could just barely see the evening star still hanging there above the trees across the river even though the moon was long up. Time was fleeting. So now he picked up his shovel and went to the pile of rocks where he'd cleared the space earlier in the evening. Enough moonlight filtered through the oaks, maples and birches to light the clearing. He got down on all fours and, using his hand as a rake, scooped the mat of leaves away from the opening in the rock pile. He was glad he'd thought to do that, for the dead leaves would help cover any part of the rock pile that seemed disturbed.

For the next two hours, Dan dug through hard scrabble, gravel, small rocks and roots. It was hard digging and his hole was anything but perfectly shaped. But Amanda was a fairly tall woman and he wanted her to lie out flat. As he had predicted the owls and whippoorwills came out to keep him company. These were sounds he'd come to trust and love. And every so often he listened carefully to see that Rex had not set up a howl at the farm. Luckily the light wind from the west didn't cut him off. He tried not to think of the worst part of his task, yet to come, but the more he attempted to bury his thoughts the more he was obsessed by the horrible thing he had to do. From time to time he cried openly, tears blinding his vision. Yet he dug on.

At last he felt that the hole was large enough since he stood to his waist in it. He must now do something he had been dreading for most of the week since he found Amanda on the beach, take her body from under the house and bury her. Just reviewing his plan made him weak in the knees and he sat on the edge of the hole dreading it...but knowing he had to do it.

Finally, he dragged himself out of the grave he'd dug, laid the shovel down on the pile of fresh dirt, and ambled slowly toward the house. He was almost spastic by the time he was inside, lifting up the trapdoor, his heart pounding. He hoped he could go through with it and ran an old Virginia spiritual through his mind as a way to reinforce his intention.

He lowered himself into the cellar area holding a lamp that he'd started with some oil borrowed from the Curtis farm. He knew he must be careful not to set his place on fire, for that would surely bring somebody running from across the river. He set the lamp down in a flat spot about three feet under the floor timbers, crawled slowly to the corner to reach Amanda's body, then crouched there for what seemed like forever until getting the courage to reach down and touch the blanket which covered her. She was certainly still there! And he hoped that the body, though beginning to smell, would hold together during the passage from cellar to grave. But he knew he couldn't think too much about that.

Strong as he was, he had difficulty pulling the shroud in which she was wrapped, dragging her across the cellar area to the trapdoor opening. As he lifted her with all his might up through the opening, he heard a thump at the front of the house. At first it scared him, then he knew what it was: a raccoon trying to get in for food. His heart pumping a little less fast, he pushed and pulled until Amanda was lying on the floor of their home.

Dan then had a tough decision to make, should he look at her dead body? What would that do to him? Could he go on if he got to sobbing again? He even imagined her live body under him and the power she had in her arms and thighs. He imagined that she was alive

still. Why was the shroud around her? Yet, how could he
live without her? take old Curtis's cranky ways? Maybe
he should crawl into the hole beside her and pull the dirt
in behind? He had heard some of his old friends in
Virginia tell about such cases where suicide was better
than heartbreak.

Again, a noise disturbed him...an acorn dropping
on the shakes with a light "Pop," one he knew by heart
since he'd listened to it so many times when he could not
sleep because Amanda was so ravishing beside him. But
the "Pop!" brought him back to his senses, and he decided
to carry Amanda to her grave without looking. "Maybe"
he thought, "I'll look just before scooping the dirt over
her?"

So he picked her up as he had on the beach and
threw her across his shoulder. She was certainly softer
than she had been coming up from the beach. He almost
literally staggered down the steps and onto the path
leading to the rock pile. And before reaching the hole he
nearly fell when he tripped over a tree root. By now the
moon was coming straight down through the overhead
branches. He knew it was full and he regarded it as a good
omen for both Amanda and him..."old companion
moon," they had called it walking up from Virginia. As
though he might hurt Amanda, he set her down very
gently.

As the enormity of his mission struck him, he
began to sob uncontrollably. So he sat on the edge of the
hole for what seemed like an eternity, feet dangling into
the grave, trying to hold his head in his hands to stop his
shaking. He heard no night sounds now, only the sound
of his heart thumping in his chest. He sat there a long
time, gradually calming, gradually regaining his sense of

the night. It was then that he knew he must see Amanda one last time.

Hesitatingly, he pulled back the shroud. Hesitatingly, he touched her skin and watched it yield to his strong fingers. Slowly, he ran his fingers along her legs, up her thighs, across her belly, around her breasts, and to her face. He traced her profile, from forehead, eyes, nose, mouth, chin, traced it slowly so he would never forget it. He also ran his fingers through her close-cropped and curly hair, did it several times. Suddenly he got an idea; he would save some pieces of her hair...as he'd saved some of his daddy's hair, kept it for good luck. So, leaving Amanda's body sunken into the darkness and barely visible in the moonlight, he ran to the house to fetch a knife. Back at her side, he carefully chopped a few strands from her head. He then looked, somewhat cautiously, at her groin. He knew how that hair felt, too, and wondered if God would forgive him if he were to take some of that hair, too. Again, he went into a sobbing fit again, lay down beside her, arm across her stomach and groin, and shook convulsively.

He did not know how long he had laid there beside her, but he knew from the position of the moon that some time had passed. Again, he got to his knees, ran his eyes and fingers over Amanda's lovely body, fantasized their sex life together, remembering the night before she disappeared. But he knew her body as sacred, and he could not violate it. What he must do was bury her, put the rocks over her, and someday discover how she died. In soft but determined whispers, he vowed, "I will avenge her death."

Putting her hair into his pocket carefully, he leaned over to kiss her soft lips one last time; they seemed to shine in the moonlight.

For just a moment he looked up into the moonlight and hummed the spiritual he most loved, "Over Jordan..."

Again, he wrapped her in the shroud he'd prepared, slipped her gently into the hole, leapt into the hole to stretch her to the hole's full length, climbed out of the grave. Taking one last look at the corner where the moonlight flooded her crumpled body, Dan picked up his shovel and slowly, but deliberately, covered her dark form. By this time he was too exhausted to cry any more. He worked as though a mechanical man, shovelful after shovelful into that black abyss...the blackest of his life. The moon was well down the west when he completed the burial, and went to work on the rock pile, to restore it to its original shape. Not until dawn did he finish; then, standing back to survey his night's work, to make sure that the rock pile looked undisturbed, he prepared to return to the Curtis barn. Though it meant going in the wrong direction, he went by way of the well and brook where he washed and stopped to look out over the awakening marsh. Remaining very quiet, he saw the doe and her fawn slip along the edge of the forest, stop, look directly at him, less than a stone's throw away, before the mother nudged her offspring's flank and entered the forest, crunching the underbrush as she went. And a flock of geese, first stirring nervously, took off with a heavy beating of wings. The noise shocked Dan for a moment. He had been so busy watching the deer he had not seen them.

Chapter VII

A Strange Intrusion

Back at the farm Dan lay down in his barn bed to rest "a few minutes." But he sank into a bottomless sleep and slept longer than he intended. By the time he was awakened by Rex's howling the sun was high in the eastern sky and the locusts had begun their hot-weather song.

Startled, Dan got up quickly to see what was happening. He knew he had been dreaming, but he didn't remember what. Was somebody coming? Were the cows in the pasture? the roosters in their pens? the pigs in the stye? It didn't take long for him to note that Rex was looking and barking toward Timber Point. Peering toward the mouth of Curtis Cove, Dan saw a dory with two men aboard. But why would Rex bark at them; he'd seen such boats before? So he stood motionless in the barn shadow to see what the men were doing. Clearly they seemed up to no good. He watched as they rowed to the far beach by the isthmus next to Little River. In a few minutes a horseman rode along the top of the dunes, hailed the men in the boat, took a bag from them, then rode off toward the forest in which Dan's cabin was located. The men in the boat shoved off and rowed back toward the mouth of the cove. Dan decided he'd best run toward his house to make sure that the man on the horse was not stopping by. So, with his usual quickness he ran down the bushy path he used as a shortcut, got to the Old Kings Highway in time to see the horseman leaving the spring where horses and wagons had watered for decades. Hidden by trees and bushes, he watched the man cross the field at the head of

Amanda's Cove, then ride along the beach past Hill's
Neck. He also saw the old horse follow the stranger with
her own eyes.

"What," Dan asked himself, "was in the bag?" He
ran his mind across all of Curtis's belongings, wondering
if the men had stolen in under cover of his sleeping? If
they got anything, what would the Curtises do to him? So
upon returning to the barn he checked out everything he
could think of to see if anything was missing. Finding
nothing gone and the house intact, he gave a sigh of relief.
He certainly didn't want to run afoul of Curtis's rotten
disposition. He took only time enough to try to fix the
horseman's face in his mind so that he might use that
information if he needed to at some later time. He then
went to work doing chores, calculating that he had
another free day before the Curtises would return.

Once he finished attending to the animals, he
picked up the hoe and went to the garden...but only after
taking a long look at the house and wondering if he dared
to defy the Curtis warning not to go in. He could not but
wonder if they had set some kind of trap for him? But he
didn't pause long wondering. He had lots to do. Curtis
would be expecting it done when he got back. He stopped
only to eat some cornbread and blueberries that he ate as
he picked.

All day he hoed and hoed. The air was heavy, only
an occasional tern screaming as it passed overhead. For
all of his brooding over last night's events, he was
thankful that the green head flies had thinned out. He
was glad for that because the pesky things stuck on all of
the bare parts of arms, legs, neck...and BIT! He was glad,
too, that Amanda was at last laid to rest...and he felt sure
that nobody would find her. But he only had to think of

her for a few moments when he would break into tears. This worried him. He must brace himself against this if working side-by-side with Curtis. Otherwise, how explain it? He began making up stories that he could use if it happened. He would blame it onto his Old Daddy, now dead and gone...or for Amanda's leaving him...or for believing he would never see any of his old plantation friends. He must simply remember to use the same explanation every time. Simply thinking about these things helped pass the time of day.

Evening came, chores completed, Rex petted, cows milked and milk put into the cooling well. After the sun went down and Dan spied the whirling beams from the Wood Island lighthouse, he decided to visit his cabin. He took the usual route, checked the door of his abode, took a long meaningful glance at the rock pile above Amanda's grave, then strolled down to the well. He sat quietly in the dark, only the faintest glow still gracing the western sky. Somewhere out on the marsh two birds squawked. He didn't know what they were, but he knew that even nature had its natural enemies. He decided at that very point in time that he would devote a few moments each twilight to thinking about Amanda's beauty. So he looked upon the evening star and gently hummed his favorite songs. He did not know how long he crouched there beside the well, but he knew he had to return to the barn to sleep.

So he drifted off to sleep that he considered "the sleep of death." In fact he dreamed of his former plantation owner's death. The man got caught in a driving blizzard, broke his leg, fell in the snow, could not get up, and perished in the cold. When Dan awoke that Sunday morning, he puzzled over the dream. It never snowed in Virginia in the summer. But maybe, Dan figured, the-cold blooded way of dealing with people finally caught up with him?

Sunday was like most every other day on the farm, with the usual chores to do. But something happened which Dan would never forget. The Curtises got home around noon rather than the time they had planned to arrive. And Ralph was not with them. Mom Curtis looked drawn, and he noticed that she had been crying. Curtis acted so strangely that Dan knew something had happened. But he dared not ask. He simply greeted them and said, "Glad you got home all right."

Curtis glowered at him, merely snapped, "Ralph's been shipped south," then took the house key from his pocket, twirling it on a string, walking almost defiantly to the porch steps and turning only to order, "Dan, bring the luggage into the house!"

Dan did as he was told, following Mrs. Curtis at a safe distance and making no effort to engage in conversation.

When all three of them got into the house, Curtis growled, "Amanda did not come back?"

"No," Dan responded, firmly but almost sheepishly.

Curtis then snapped, "Ralph's not here to help. Mrs. Curtis and I are getting old. We've hired a girl from an up-country farm. She'll be coming next Saturday when she finishes work in the mill. I want you to help her with whatever she needs."

That was one of the longest speeches he'd ever heard Curtis give, but he said, simply, "Yas suh." And returned to the barn to finish what was expected of him on any Sunday.

As he worked, however, he wondered: Amanda had been gone less than a month, but Curtis was replacing her. Did Curtis know more than he? What would another person mean or do to the farm? Who was this girl? How might her presence change his life? Even as Curtis came to the barn, gave Rex a kick, and began to use abusive language to Dan, Dan was finding this new knowledge puzzling. Nor did he have any better idea of what might have happened to Amanda. And he had to bite his tongue and hold his fists tight when Curtis took a bottle from his secret hiding place, began to drink, then started to call Amanda all of the names he could find in his vocabulary, "Bitch, whore, witch, lazy, good-for-nothing nigger..." Dan knew that he could not become angry or strike Curtis without risking his own situation and life. So he kept at his chores, silently, even as Curtis's voice climbed higher and higher.

In a half hour or so Curtis was staggering about, treating the poor hound even more wretchedly and beginning to swear about his wife, calling her names and complaining, "bitch...ungrateful..no sex...headaches, headaches, headaches...!" Again, Dan treated Curtis remarks with silence...until finally Curtis turned on him, sending a whole string of expletives in his direction. Dan was tempted to hit him with a nearby shovel but resisted. Of course, Dan's silence made Curtis the angrier, and he finally said, "And you're a worthless nigger, too, my property, a no-good! Why don't you defend yourself to prove you're a man?"

Dan thought carefully, quietly responding, "Because I have nothing to say. You know the work I do."

Dan had seen Curtis this way once or twice before, the day Ralph went off to the war, the same night the calf was stillborn. He knew that it was useless to answer him. That would make him worse. But Dan kept his distance in case Curtis got violent and swung a fist or shovel at him.

In a few moments he heard Mom Curtis call to Curtis. "Shut up, John! Come in here and go to bed." Dan had never heard her talk to him like this, but her command seemed to work. The farmer turned abruptly, took another futile swing at the dog and staggered off to the house, falling up the porch steps to land squarely on his face. He lay there for a moment. Mrs. Curtis brought him a glass of water, forced it into him, then helped him up. Together they staggered into the kitchen.

Dan paused a moment, completed his chores, then walked slowly home, reflecting upon these recent events. What had really triggered Curtis' anger and drinking? Amanda's death? Ralph's leaving? His wife's nagging? What?

Chapter VIII

The New Girl

The following Saturday afternoon, Jeannette Scamman, accompanied by her father and older brother, reached the Curtis farm. Dan was clearing annual growth along the main lane when their wagon rolled in from North Saco. Dan stopped swinging the scythe for a moment, stared. Henry Scamman stopped the horse, and he and his son stared back. Dan then heard the father say to his offspring, "Look, there's the farmhand Curtis told us about! But look, he's BLACK!"

Dan went back to work before the wagon continued toward the barn, but he felt in his bones that Scamman's remark boded no good. Not long afterward he heard the two men greet one another in the barnyard, and soon he heard them arguing loudly. While he couldn't make out every word, he did hear them say "Nigger" again and again. It seemed fairly clear that Scamman felt that Curtis had misled him by not telling him Dan's color. Soon things were quiet again; the two families had gone into the house. He heard only the waves pounding hard against the sides of Curtis Cove. So he kept swinging the scythe and mulling over his encounter with the Scamman family. Every so often he found himself licking his lips, salty from sweat and the salt-filled air. He was also careful to relieve himself behind bushes so as not to be visible from the house.

An hour or so passed, and he waited with some fear about what might happen next. Finally, after what seemed an eternity, he heard Scamman and Curtis say their good-byes and the horse snorted a little as the wagon started back down the lane. Dan didn't miss a stroke in his scything rhythms, but he deliberately turned his back to the lane. Likewise, he could tell by the sounds that the Scammanses wanted no further encounter and passed right by his workspace.

Dan worked his usual time, until the blistering sun was low in the sky, then stuck his whetstone in his hip pocket, put the scythe over his shoulder and walked slowly back to the barn. As he hung up the scythe and put the stone in its place on the eye-high shelf, he heard the house door open and saw Curtis out of the corner of his eye walking briskly across the narrow porch heading in his direction. But Dan made no unusual moves, simply prepared to put the rest of his tools away and go home.

As Curtis entered the barn, he asked, "Did you see the Scamman family?"

"Yes, suh," Dan responded, respectfully.

"Did you hear us talking?"

"No suh," Dan said, protectively.

"Well," Curtis continued, "Henry Scamman was disturbed about your color. He thought I said you were white. But he must have assumed it, for all I ever told him was that you were a good worker."

Dan said nothing, simply stood his ground and stared at the tall farmer.

Curtis seemed uncomfortable and uncertain about what to say next. Dan kept staring at him, not really

caring how uncomfortable he felt.   After all, it wasn't his
problem? or would it be?

Finally, Curtis scowled a little, sputtered under his
breath and went on.   "I told him you were married to
Amanda, that Amanda had gone away several weeks ago.
Scamman made me promise that you would have
nothing to do with his daughter except talk about
household work.   I promised him, and now you must
promise me!   And if anything else happens, I'll kick your
ass as quickly as I would kick Rex!"

He paused a moment, then remarked, "Incidentally
her name is Jeannette but she wants to be called 'Nett.' If
you talk with her, you are to use that name."

Dan said, "Yes suh."   He knew that Curtis was a
man of his word, and he had seen the result on the poor
old hound.   Yet he also knew that Curtis had done unto
him what he said he would do, providing the shack,
providing meals, providing work.   Also he had just called
him a good worker. So much as he hated the man, he had
to comply.   After a few moments, he said, "No problem, I
still want Amanda to come back."

As he spoke Amanda's name, he looked directly
into Curtis's eyes to see if he could catch any clues to
confirm his suspicion that Curtis may have been
involved in foul play.   But he saw only that Curtis had
avoided his glance, turned his head, and looked out on
the cove.   Curtis shuffled his feet a bit, then shouted
nervously, almost at the top of his voice, "Then, it's
settled. I'll see you tomorrow."

Dan's walk home was filled with many questions,
ones he'd asked himself over and over.   He could not tell

all that was going on. What were Curtis's intentions? Why did he persist in speaking as though Amanda might show up if he knew that Amanda was dead? As he thrashed and turned on his bed, trying to overcome the discomfort of hot and sticky weather, such questions continued to pester him deep into the night.

****

The next few days were rather tense. He knew that Curtis was watching him like a hawk. He observed Nett Scamman from a distance. She was a comely lass, medium height with molasses colored hair, pulled back tight into a bun at the nape of her neck. "In many ways," Dan mused, "she was shaped like Amanda." She seemed to work hard, attended to Mrs. Curtis hand and foot. She rarely came to the barn or to the fields where Dan and Curtis were attending to late summer harvest. Once when Curtis was in town shopping she asked help moving some canning crocks from the cellar to the kitchen. Mom Curtis hovered over her like a mother hen so they did not talk.

And each night was the same agony for Dan, wondering about Amanda deep under those rocks. Each night he sat at the well, watching the stars or the moon and listening to owls and night hawks as well as Old Smith, his dog and wife across the marsh. Occasionally he saw a dim light, probably a lantern, in front of Smith's barn and saw his huge shadow flit across the barn door as he passed between lantern and barn. He looks like a giant, Dan thought...and such a tiny man, too. Sometimes Dan knew that he was drunk for the shadow staggered.

After the first frost, Dan set up another evening routine for himself. He followed the bouldered shoreline of Amanda's Cove and walked to the end of Bayberry Point where he could look east to see the Wood Island light flash or to the west to see similar flashes down the Coast. He didn't know what to call the ones to the west. Nobody had ever told him. But he found comfort in those lights, just as he figured that sailors found comfort in keeping them from crashing on the rocks and reefs. He wondered how they could see or hear these warnings during a storm or in the thick fogs which sometimes set in for entire days. One night he watched the fog drift in and out of the Cove in the moonlight, eerie, like the white scarf Amanda used for her hair, blowing in the wind. He also tasted the heavy salt on his lips, and it had a way of making him feel at home.

But from his perch on the highest rock on Bayberry Point he could also look across the narrow coves to see the Curtis house. Usually the house was dark as he looked. But sometimes when all four rooms to the east were lighted with lamps, the old grey house looked as festive as the old plantation house he knew growing up as a boy. Yet, he was sure that having fun was not in Curtis's nature. He could only speculate why the lamps were so bright in the first place. "Perhaps," he thought, "it has something to do with Nett Scamman's presence? or maybe Curtis and his wife have taken up reading?" He simply did not know, but he did enjoy climbing to his perch and watching...especially during full moonlit nights. He also enjoyed the fresh sea smells which blew across the point, especially after a day of lugging seaweed from the beaches or dung from the manure pile...all for the gardens.

One morning following the September full moon Dan showed up at the barn to find Curtis already there.

Speaking firmly, he asked Dan, "Did you spend all night on Bayberry Point?"

"No, suh!"

"You lie!" Curtis exclaimed, "I saw you there in the moonlight."

"Yas, suh, I was there for a little while but not all night."

This seemed to calm Curtis a little, but he let forth with a barrage of questions. "But after working hard all day, what do you do out there on my rocks? Don't you need to rest to be ready for work? What's there to attract you? And who said you could go there?"

The barrage confused Dan a little. What to say? But after a brief pause and a deep breath, he responded, "I like the moon on the watuh. It makes me think of Amanda." He secretly hoped he'd have to say no more.

"Can't get her off your mind, can you?"

"No suh." And he forced back the tears.

Curtis said no more and went about doing his part of the chores. Dan looked up to see Nett Scamman approaching but continued with his work.

Nett walked into the barn rather briskly, said, "Good morning, Dan," then turned immediately to Curtis. "Mrs. Curtis is sick," she announced. "You must come quickly," turned and ran for the house.

Dan watched her run and noticed how graceful she was as Curtis muttered something under his breath and walked firmly across the barnyard to the kitchen door.

Dan began to hear shouting from the house so knew that Mom Curtis was arguing with her husband.

Half the morning passed. It was chilly, and the Almanac called for frost. Dan knew they had to cover some of the plants that afternoon or lose the late vegetables, so he set about preparing for that task. Around noon Curtis found Dan working in the garden, and Dan initiated the conversation in the hope he could get Curtis off his back.

"How's Mrs. Curtis?"

"Not well!" Curtis grumped.

Dan said no more but watched Curtis out of the corner of his eye. Still no clues about Mom Curtis or Amanda.

Finally Curtis said, "It's a risk, but we've got to take her to town to see a doctor. And you will come with us because I can't leave Nett alone with you. You can ride in the back of the wagon as far as my cousin's in South Biddeford. I'll leave you there in the barn until we can see the doctor. Be ready to go early afternoon. Wear the best clothes you've got in case anybody sees you. Don't you have that old jacket I wore out last year?"

"Yes suh," Dan responded as casually as he could but with his heart pounding from the uncertainty of the new experience and the unknown.

On his way to his house he mused, "So Curtis is going to take me to town for the first time in all these years? He must be scared of something. Why not take Nett and leave me here; he's left me lots of times before?"

But he knew he had to obey or perhaps lose his house, job, and place beside Amanda. He was at once excited to be able to see more of the territory. But he was also frightened. More questions raced through his mind: "Was this Curtis's way of turning him over to the sheriff and accuse him of Amanda's death? And where did his cousin live? How long would they be gone?"

But he did as he was told, for he did not want to cross Curtis. He put on the old threadbare jacket, ate a piece of cornbread that he'd made the night before, turned around and started back to the barn. As he passed Amanda's burial cairn, he almost whispered aloud, "I'll be right back."

Chapter IX

To Town

Arriving back at the barn he harnessed up the old horse and held the reins while Curtis and Nett helped Mom Curtis into the wagon. Dan observed that she did not look well, but he said nothing. Curtis got into the wagon, grabbed the reins and held the horse while Dan climbed onto the tailboard.

"Hold on!" Curtis commanded, and they waved good-bye to Nett. "Be back by dark," Curtis explained. "Nothing to worry about."

Nett merely signaled her understanding with a quick raising of her hand, her long hair blowing in the wind. Dan remained motionless.

Sitting on the tailboard of the open wagon, Dan was thankful it was not raining. Also it gave him a chance to think and observe without being observed. He'd not seen any of the country beyond Hill's Neck or the marsh. He enjoyed the trees, for they had begun to turn red, yellow and rust colors. And even looking back at the gravel road with its long grey stone walls on either side had its appeal. He also enjoyed hearing the horse's hooves and steelbanded wheels bite into the gravel. The sounds carried their own rhythms and almost put him to sleep. The Curtises talked very little, but even the words he heard, "sick," "medicine," "impossible," "liquor," "when," "where," "Nett," didn't tell him very much. Once they even mentioned "Amanda." Dan turned toward the front of the wagon, hoping to hear more, but the Curtises were staring directly ahead. He still couldn't figure out what was going on.

They had been on the road for some time when Dan felt the wagon lurch and knew they'd turned off. He twisted his head to see that they were entering a lane to another farm. "This must be the cousin's place," he thought. In a few moments they were stopping in front of an old weather-beaten, broken down house with a barn sporting a huge hole in the roof. In fact, Dan stared so steadily at the hole that Curtis caught him and looked himself but said nothing. He got out of the wagon, but Mrs. Curtis sat bolt upright on the seat. "Stay where you are, Dan!" Curtis commanded, "I'll be right back."

He turned and went into the barn, strolling back a few moments later with a ragged, shaggy man with a long graying beard, a man Dan thought must be ten to twenty years older than Curtis. When nearly to the wagon the older man sort of tipped his straw hat to Mrs. Curtis, said "Hello," but kept walking until he stood only a few feet from Dan, nearly face to face.

"Dan, this is my cousin Amos," Curtis observed, matter of factly.

"Howdy," Dan said, keeping his reserve as protection.

"Dan, you're gonna stay with Amos until Mrs. Curtis and I come back from the doctor's. Don't you dare to stir from the barn or you'll get a beating!"

Dan knew he didn't intend to stir, but simply nodded.

Slipping down off the tailboard, he followed the two men into the old decaying barn. Curtis continued his instructions, "And, Dan, I want no talking about anything happening at the Curtis farm. Amos here is deaf and almost blind, and I'll tell him what I want him to know. Right now, you are to be quiet."

"Yes suh, Mr. Curtis," Dan obliged.

He then watched Curtis return to the wagon, turn it around, saw Amos shade his eyes from the bright afternoon sun, then watched the wagon roll down the lane.

Amos steered Dan to a neighboring hay mow and invited him to sit down and rest while he "fetched" a cup of water from the well behind the barn. Again, Dan did as he was told; but while the old man was gone, he stood up to look around...saw that he could see the blue sky through the hole in the roof, observed that Amos couldn't have more than a couple of cows, saw no evidence of pigs or horses, heard a few hens clucking in the yard. "He doesn't have much," Dan thought. "He must be what he'd heard Curtis call 'a poor relation.'" He then sat down before Amos returned with water and a piece of hard tack such as sailors took to sea.

As he took the water and cracker, Dan felt pretty sure that Amos would be pumping him to see what was happening. Sure enough he hadn't eaten half of it before Amos began.

"Do you like living at the Curtis farm, Dan?"

"Yes suh." He dared not say anything else.

"Do you work hard?"

"Yes, suh." He figured that this old Yankee valued hard work so told Amos what he thought he wanted to hear.

"Do you have other black friends or family around the farm?"

This was more difficult to answer, for he didn't know what Curtis might have told Amos? So he simply said, "I'm married."

Amos paused a moment, seeming to be unwilling to carry that line of discussion any further, then asked, "Have you ever seen the Saco River?"

"No, suh," Dan replied.

"Then let's go see it," Amos proposed.

"But Mr. Curtis told me to stay in the barn," Dan observed, starting to feel uneasy again. "Was this a trap or a test?"

"Oh, it will be all right. John's not close by, and the river's just behind the barn. We can see it from the ramp going down to the field."

Dan felt even more uncomfortable disobeying Curtis, for he knew that Curtis could be brutal if crossed. So somewhat reluctantly he let himself be led to the back of the barn where, indeed, he could see the river flowing to the sea. "Pretty!" he exclaimed. "Where does it go?"

"Do you know where the lighthouse is?" Amos asked.

"I seen it flash at night," Dan responded.

"All right," Amos smiled even as he spit a long squirt of tobacco juice, just missing Dan and almost hitting the chicken pen.

He chuckled as he saw Dan recoil from the spitting, but continued, "The river goes into the ocean just this side of the lighthouse."

And thus the afternoon passed, Amos trying to probe Dan for information about the farm after enticing him to have another biscuit, walk to the river bank, and engage in general conversation. But Dan was too cautious to be caught. Also, he knew he must be back in that barn when Curtis returned from the doctor's...or else he might get a beating when they got home. As time dragged his heart beat a little faster. He didn't expect Curtis to be gone so long. When the wagon finally rolled into the yard just before sunset, Curtis was all apologies to his cousin. As he handed Amos a gift plug of tobacco, he explained, "Had to wait for the doctor to come back from delivering a baby. Also decided to get some grain while waiting. Save me a trip."

Dan could see the bags piled in the back of the wagon and knew he'd have to unload them when they got home.

Amos, feeling a bit on the friendly side and decidedly relieved that Curtis was back, volunteered, "I showed Dan the river, but we kept back of the bushes, nobody seed us."

Curtis flushed and started, "I thought I told you, Dan, to...."

But Amos cut him off, "No harm done to let the black man see some of the world. We stood in the shadows. I told you nobody seed us."

Curtis said nothing.

Then Amos remarked, "It's late. Wanta stay all night?"

Mom Curtis spoke up and said, "No thanks, Amos, but I'm tired. I want to go home and sleep in my own bed. Next time we come to town." She sensed that Amos was being polite and did not really want to sleep under the same roof with a nigger.

That concluded the amenities. Dan thanked Amos profusely for the biscuits and the tour. The Curtises waved good-bye, and they all set off in the wagon down the road. This time Dan rode on the bags of grain and admitted to himself that it was more comfortable than the bare tailboard.

They hadn't been on the road more than a half hour when night set in. The moon was not up so they knew they were on the road only by listening to the horses hooves on the gravel and by looking up to see a kind of star road through the opening in the trees. Dan had walked on such roads and paths many times to give him direction so he felt perfectly at home...though he wished he had worn more. It was getting pretty cold. To take his mind off being chilly he counted the big stars he could see and measured the number of hand widths one was from the other and how far they were from the North Star which trailed the wagon.

A few times it was pretty scarey to hear noises he'd not heard before. One seemed to be a kind of whistle behind them. And when it went off, Curtis turned to explain, "That's the curfew whistle at the York Mills."

Dan didn't quite understand, but said, "Yes suh."

A few moments later he heard a noise on the river which must have been a boat, for Amos had said that two coal and cotton boats were due on the high tide this evening. When he heard the noise again, Curtis turned and said, "Boats taking coal and cotton to the mills."

Dan almost felt grateful to Curtis for explaining the new sounds. He had seen these schooners on the horizon off the farm point, but they'd always glided by so silently he did not know they whistled while making their way up river.

The trip back to the farm seemed endless. Mrs. Curtis complained several times when they hit bumps or ruts that jolted the wagon. Curtis was almost civil, too, but still Dan got little sense of what was wrong with her. Finally he recognized the silhouettes around the marsh, the forest in which he lived, the stone walls along the old Kings Highway, and the turn into the main lane.

Dan was really shocked though when Curtis stopped the wagon and said, "No need to come to the barn with us. I'll take care of the horse and we can unload the grain in the morning. You've had a long day, why don't you go directly home?"

Although caught off guard, Dan did not protest. He said thanks in his own way, and slipped silently into the woodsy path leading to his house.

In a few moments he was lighting his lamp and climbing into bed to get warm....thankful for his experience but still very puzzled by Curtis' behavior.

The next day Curtis was still fairly civil. They unloaded the grain bags together, did the chores without much fuss. Dan didn't know why this was happening since it was not like Curtis to be pleasant more than a few moments in any given day. But he kept his guard high, ready for whatever might happen.

Chapter X

Paths to Winter

During the following days and weeks, leading to winter, he did make some observations that made sense. Mom Curtis spent many hours wrapped in warm blankets and sitting in the sun on the lea side of the house. Curtis said the doctor told her to get plenty of fresh air. Nett seemed to like it there at the farm, was always pleasant, and bounced from chore to chore as though happy with her work. Only once, however, did she ever say anything to Dan about working there. She was working beside Mrs. Curtis combing out some sheep's wool that a neighbor had traded for some squash. Dan was trying to fix a window, one that had leaked badly during a recent southeast storm. Nett looked up, caught his eye, then as though speaking to Mom Curtis, said, "This is so much more fun than piecing up the ends at the York."

Dan didn't know what "piecing up the ends" meant so he ventured an inquiry, "What is 'piecing up the ends,' Maam?"

Nett cheerfully explained what happened when cotton threads came through the rollers on the spinning machines and were spun and twisted onto a spindle, how they broke between rollers and spindles, and how young women such as herself were hired by the York, Laconia and Pepperell Mills to tie the broken threads together.

Dan listened carefully, not fully understanding what she was saying, but liking to hear her voice. And he enjoyed watching her long thin hands as she enacted the piecing-up process. She was such a pleasant change from Curtis's usual gruff tones and demeanor.

After he'd thanked her as "Miz Scamman," she said, "All right, but my name is Nett, Dan; you don't have to be so formal. No matter what my father made you and Mr. Curtis promise, we both work here."

Unthinkingly, Dan said, "Yes, Maam," then along with Mom Curtis, they laughed.

Nett went on carding wool with Mrs. Curtis, who had said nothing but carefully watched the brief exchange between Dan and Nett. Dan returned to his leak-plugging job, enjoying the sunshine out of the wind and in the protection of the building. Upon finished his work, he went directly back to the tool shed, fearing that Curtis might have seen them talking and expecting the worse if he had.

But Curtis was nowhere to be seen so Dan put the tools away and went about his next chore, savoring the brief discussion with Nett and wishing he could visit the Biddeford and Saco mills Nett talked about and see other sights in town. But he knew in his heart of hearts that Curtis didn't want to be seen with him nor to have him seen. So he quickly put that thought away and got down to more of the farm harvesting. Also he watched the tide, for he knew he had to dig "a mess of clams" before the afternoon was over. Curtis said, "The house is planning steamers for supper."

Just a few days later he was on his way home when he suddenly crossed from the back bushy path into the Kings Highway and almost ran into Nett returning to the house from an early cranberrying expedition. He apologized for almost bumping into her and continued on his way. But she called him back.

"Dan," she said, "Did you know that my brother was here visiting me today? He had business with Farmer Smith across the marsh so I went over to see him. Also he brought down some clippings about farming that he thought Mr. Curtis might like."

"Yes, ma--, I mean, Nett, I saw them working at the edge of the marsh."

"I want to tell you that he and my father have gotten used to my speaking of you whenever I see them. I don't think you have to worry about talking with me."

Dan wrinkled his forehead a little but remained silent. He was more fearful of Curtis than the Scamman family. But Nett continued.

"You know my family hasn't seen more than a half dozen black people in their entire lives. They know that a war is being fought over black folk and slavery, but they don't understand that black folk are people such as you. They were upset to see you when they brought me down here, 'cause they think that Curtis deceived them and they've heard all kinds of stories about black people being animals. I know those stories are not true, just as you know they aren't true. So please don't worry about speaking with me. This is a lonely enough place without each of us living in our own cell, almost captives of John Curtis. Mrs. Curtis is different; she likes both of us."

Still Dan remained silent.

Nett explained, "I've spoken to Mom Curtis about telling you this and she is supposed to talk with her husband. I think it is going to be all right."

Dan felt strange and a bit uneasy, for he had seen Curtis's wrath and didn't want a lash on his back or a kick in the rear. So he edged away toward the path leading to his house and left her with a simple "Thank you, Ma--, I mean Nett."

They both smiled and went their respective ways.

Dan sat in his rocker and rocked steadily that evening. He hoped that Curtis would not take it out on him for violating the promise he made. He kinda liked Nett. He had never met anybody like her before, seeming to care for people, seeming as fresh as the morning dew on the marsh. Best of all, she reminded him of Amanda. She was tall, strong, pleasant. And, of course, Dan could not think about Amanda without reviewing their lives from the time they first met until that last fateful night when he buried her in the moonlight.

The autumn leaves fell and turned to dust under his feet. He prepared for winter by banking the lower sides of his little house, just as he did with the big house at the farm. Leaves, evergreen branches, grass...all packed tightly to keep the cold winds and freezing weather out. As he worked on the banking chores, he kept hoping that heavy snow would fall early this year and keep the ground from freezing too deep. Also that would seal the banking materials quickly and keep his cabin warmer. He had learned all these little tricks of survival from Curtis and he felt good about what he knew about farm work...certainly different than it was on the tobacco plantation in Virginia.

Also he knew that snow covering the rocks over Amanda's grave might reduce the chance that a stray animal might dig there. Still he was not sure?

He also watched and listened to the huge flocks of giant geese fly over the farm and ocean. Sometimes they seemed to skim the water, at other times the chimneys. Curtis once surprised him by explaining that the geese must have spent the night in the marshes near Biddeford Pool and were having a difficult time gaining altitude for their trip south. At other times they were very high, and he enjoyed watching them shift leaders at those heights. For all he knew each was a leader; sometimes it seemed that way. Even Curtis would stop to look, but he could not figure out why Curtis took scraps of paper from his pocket to write something down about them. Maybe he was counting them? Maybe he was recording the time of day? Dan didn't dare ask what or why he was doing this.

One day, though, Curtis asked right out of a clear blue sky, "Dan, ever heard of Ben Franklin? or John Audubon?"

"No suh," Dan responded, dutifully.

"Well," said Curtis, standing tall but leaning on his shovel and gazing back and forth across the sky, "Franklin was a kind of scientist and experimented with lightning. Audubon studied and painted birds. Someday somebody is going to be asking about the habits of these birds. I'm piling up facts about them. Incidentally, lightning struck and burned houses in Buxton last month, and you know how we fear it here!"

Dan was fascinated but he dared not say anything. Curtis detected his interest and continued to talk.

"Maybe you've seen me with all of those papers when I come back from town. Some of those papers are scientific, and there's some talk about forming a scientific society soon. It will study and collect data from all York County. If it happens, I may join."

"Good, suh," was all that Dan could muster. He still disliked and mistrusted the man so knew he had to be careful about what he said even though he felt that he knew quite a bit about nature.

The day passed. More birds flew south, long, scraggly flocks of them, and Curtis spent more time writing notes than shoveling black muck in the ditch they were expanding to drain his holdings on the marsh.

A little later while resting on his shovel, Curtis again caught Dan's ear and began to lecture. "I've been reading the farming articles Nett's brother brought me the other day. Good stuff on the history of the tomato and composting wood ashes and muck. I think we can use some of those ideas right here next summer and improve our products. Maybe we can enter some of our vegetables in the Fair another year."

Dan listened intently because he had no choice. Nor could he deny that what Curtis was saying was interesting. Since he could not read himself, Curtis at least gave him a viewpoint and information which he might not otherwise have.

As he dug without further interruption and later that night while chewing spruce gum, reflectively by his stove, he wondered where the geese went? Why did they go so regularly in the spring and fall? How did they know when to come back? Did God tell them? He even

wondered if the songs he sang applied to them as much as
to his people?   And why did plants grow to produce food
they could eat?   And later that evening as the winds
began howling around his cabin door, he wondered about
wonder? Why did he ask why? And was there anybody
anywhere who could answer such questions? He knew
that his old daddy had the wisdom of his people and
answered such questions by telling stories or singing
spirituals.   Was there anybody in this godforsaken
northland who did the same thing?

****

Autumn blended into winter. The nights got very
cold, and sometimes when the wood supply was low or
the wind drove hard down the chimney, Dan couldn't get
a good fire going. So he went to bed early to stay warm
under a great pile of blankets. He liked those nights, for it
gave him time to reminisce. He would never forget one
night.

Actually he was rocking beside the stove, sort of
dozing off. Reminiscence became fantasy which became a
dream. He was walking toward a brightly-lighted, high-
porticoed southern home. As he walked up the steps,
Amanda came running toward him as three little white
girls greeted him by shouting in unison, "Welcome
home, massah." Amanda hugged and kissed him, poked
him all over to test the reality of his being present. And as
he walked into his house, a chorus of black children began
to sing his favorite spiritual about "goin' home!" He felt
tears running down his cheeks...when suddenly he heard
a bump on his little cottage roof and saw the end of a limb
sticking through. The lamp was dim, but it began to
flicker as the wind blew down through the house. He
leapt up quickly and climbed into the rafters to push the

branch back out onto the roof until he could fix it in the morning and put a patch over the hole to keep out the wind.

As he sat back into his favorite chair and felt the warmth of the stove, now sporting two bright red spots in its sides, he was thankful to be warm. But the dream puzzled him. Why had he dreamt that HE was master of a Virginia plantation? and what did it mean? And what did it mean to have a limb come through his roof just as he broke into tears. Was God trying to punish him for reaching too high? Were these evil omens? The tears were so real he put his fingers up to his eyes to see if they were still there. By this time, of course, his eyes were dry from all of the climbing about to fix the roof.

So fall became winter. The last little egret left the marsh. Pockets of fresh water from the fall rains froze. His well skimmed over every day, and he had to break the ice to fetch his daily pail. After one storm he found Farmer Jesse and his sons digging quahogs on Amanda's Beach. The tide was very low and their pails filling rapidly. He was tempted to walk down to speak to them but decided not to. Curtis might not like it.

But after each storm he spent "free" time collecting drift wood for the fence he was building around his little cabin; he also wondered if it might be a good idea to surround Amanda's grave with such a fence? It might keep off the animals? He enjoyed those strolls along the beach because he never knew what he might find, an unusual shell, a stray fish or lobster that he could take to the farm or cook himself. On unusually low tides he also dug quahogs for the dinner table, and he loved the chowders that Mom Curtis and Nett made.

Curtis seemed to be taking the wagon to town more frequently, leaving Dan to do more chores alone. This didn't bother Dan, for he felt more comfortable working by himself, even on back-breaking jobs such as building stone walls or digging clams in the river than he did with Curtis along beside him. For days at a time he never saw Mom Curtis...though he did continue to enjoy the home cooking she sent to the barn via Nett almost every day. Seeing Nett was always pleasing. They spoke to one another more naturally now, and he felt comfortable calling her by name. Once Curtis heard them address one another by familiar first names, seemed a bit startled, but said nothing. Dan figured that Mom Curtis and Nett must have spoken to him about the promise. Yet, Dan always kept his guard up; for even at his most pleasant, Curtis's voice was gruff enough to plough ground.

Dan also felt good about some carpentry jobs which Curtis laid out, remodeling the stable and adding a shed between house and barn. It gave Dan focus and took his mind off everyday things. While he hated to work in the teeth of bitter winds off the ocean, still that was better than testing Curtis's temper. Dan acknowledged that Curtis had taught him well the basic skills of carpentry, and he was always careful to follow Curtis's instructions.

Dan had difficulty believing that he was invited to spend Thanksgiving Day in the barn where he could partake of the good food Nett and Mom Curtis had cooked. True, it was not at their table, but it was better than cooking his own meal. In fact, it was one of the few times he'd seen Mrs. Curtis in the barn. She and Nett, lugging two plates of food apiece, brought him his dinner about noon...just as they said they would. He remembered the big brown and red rooster that he'd had to kill for the dinner; yet, that memory didn't curb his appetite! He also remembered the other vegetables he'd helped raise and was thankful for several things: that Nett had arrived to lighten the atmosphere; that they remembered he had helped raise the food; that Amanda was safe in her grave and not being eaten up by crabs, lobsters and preying fish. Having these thoughts to mull over while eating his meal, he could tolerate the lack of human company...even as he remembered his and Amanda's Thanksgiving meal in their home and making love beside the warm fire after dinner the year before. He was also thankful that Curtis had decided not to come to the barn with any of the food.

Upon finishing his dinner, he shared a few leftovers with Rex, then neatly piled the dishes on the porch steps before walking slowly down the bushy pathway toward home.

Since Curtis had given Dan the afternoon off and he didn't have to report back until evening chores, he decided to walk along the shore to his lookout on Bayberry Point. He took his time, picked up a few smooth rocks small enough to slip into his pocket and add to his collection and occasionally skipped a flat one across the calm water. He also saw carcasses of horseshoe crabs, a few lobster and crab bodies, pieces of bone that seem to come from fish or small animals. He picked up one of the larger pieces, thinking he might be able to carve something from it. Crossing the little bog that lay between the smaller coves, he even found a couple of cranberries which he must have missed a few weeks before when he came out for the annual harvest. Almost instinctively, he put them into his mouth despite the fact that he'd just had a good meal. But he quickly spit them out, they were so sour.

When he finally reached his perch on the big rock, he stood for a long time to take in the seascape and enjoy. He saw a flock of eiders swimming in Amanda's cove, ploughing along as though in a squadron. He wondered if they ever formed V's like the geese? Seagulls were diving for fish off shore. He thought he saw a whale spout in the vicinity of the diving gulls but wasn't quite sure although he scanned the surface in all directions from that spot. He also enjoyed the clouds, big and puffy; they reminded him of cotton he'd once picked on a neighbor's plantation in Virginia. It was a cold day, but almost perfect to see as far as the eye could reach along the whole ocean front.

He'd been there a long time, so long he even sat down on the board he'd once brought out from the house to make it more comfortable . Softer, certainly than sitting on hard rock. He was looking toward the southeast, out past Timber Island toward Cape Porpoise as he had many times before when his eye caught something moving on Curtis Point. Remaining motionless but letting his eye wander toward the Curtis house, he saw a figure moving from house to the point. It was Nett. He watched her for a long time. She, too, stood on a high boulder and studied the sea. After awhile she seemed to spot him and waved...a bit reluctantly at first then with a more positive motion as though wanting him to wave back. At first he wasn't quite sure what to do; Curtis's wrath still controlled his view to the world. But when Nett continued to wave, he finally returned the greeting, also expanding it from a hesitant half-wave to a fuller recognition of her signal.

Dan continued to watch her move into the house. The event added to the warmth of the sun. "Another human being on that lonely piece of coast," he thought, "almost a miracle." He almost flew back to his house, his heart beating rapidly from the shock of recognition.

******

December was a fairly mild month, but it was marked by the first snow storm. It began spitting in early afternoon as Dan and Curtis worked on a new stonewall running perpendicularly from the King's Highway toward the farm house. Curtis said he wanted to experiment with a new breed of pig next spring and thought he'd put them in a separate stye. At first the driving snowflakes didn't bother them very much. What they were doing was hot work so they had stripped down to one layer of clothing. They could see their own breath, fog clouds near their mouths. But they worked on, rolling huge boulders, some of them so heavy they had to use bars and all their strength to move them into place for the base of the wall. Doing such chores brought Dan shoulder to shoulder with the gruff old farmer, even to the point of touching. Dan felt the resistances to such touching, but knew he could do nothing about it. They needed joint strength...even when they rolled such rocks onto the horse-drawn sledge. By midafternoon the wind was so strong and the snow so thick, they were experiencing a full-scale blizzard. Finally, Curtis said, "Enough of this, let's go home."

They carried their tools back to the barn, did some of the evening chores early, then went their respective ways.

Dan was both fascinated and angered by the snow. He did things which Maine kids had done for generations, holding his face toward the wind, opening his mouth and catching snowflakes on his tongue...only to feel them melt. He also enjoyed watching the trees filter the wind and snow until the woods filled up with flakes. But there was the other side of the storm; he knew it meant back-breaking work shoveling, hiking back and forth to the barn in knee-deep snow that would wet him to the skin and chill him to the bone. Also, he now had Amanda's cairn to watch. With no snow on the ground, her grave stood a stark gray against the black tree trunks and leaf-carpeted ground. Now he could see for the first time that her grave would be indistinguishable from the surrounding whiteness of the forest. This worried him a little. Should he thrust a stick into the pile of stones to mark its place? or mark it some other way? He wasn't too sure but finally decided to do nothing to call attention to the rock pile. Somebody might stumble in and begin asking questions.

The night of the first storm did give him the opportunity, however, to sit by the fire, close his eyes and try to dream again of that huge Virginia plantation house and all those beautiful children and songs. He dozed and dozed and dozed, but no dreams came. All he could hear was the wind howling in the trees overhead. Also, a hoot owl set up a clatter in the old hollow tree he'd almost chopped down for firewood until he discovered birds occupying it. Failing to dream the pleasant dream, he banked the fire early and sought refuge in bed.

Later on, he seemed to remember that it was the day after the first storm that he saw something unusual happening at the house. He heard Curtis and his wife shouting at one another "somethin' awful." He was milking the cows on the house side of the barn and didn't catch every word, but he could tell that the argument was fierce. He imagined all kinds of scenarios, but didn't have much to go on, until...

He looked up to see Nett trying to escape through the kitchen door. But just as she was about to slip through, Curtis grabbed her by the wrist and jerked her back into the house. No more. He saw no more than that. But it did appear that Curtis was abusing her. Although Dan was tempted to rush to the house and thrash Curtis if necessary, he sat at the milking stool and continued to strip the cows to their last drop.

Shortly afterward Curtis came to the barn to do his routine chores and was very quiet the rest of the day, never once mentioning what had happened. Dan, too, remained silent, knowing well that nothing good could happen if he opened his mouth. He only wished that he could talk with Nett and find out what happened. But silence reigned, and he did not get one glimpse of her or Mom Curtis for the balance of the day.

The next morning, a Friday as Dan recalled later, Curtis announced that he and Dan would leave for town around noon to go for grain, mail and other goods. "And this time, Dan, you're not going to stop with Amos; you're going to go with me to help with the work I have to do. Also, we'll be gone two or three days."

This shocked Dan. It threatened to upset his routine and security. Somewhat hesitantly, he asked, "But you didn't want me to be seen. I'm black!"

"I know, but I have good news for you. Word has reached Maine that Abraham Lincoln is about to announce an Emancipation Proclamation the first of the year."

"Ralph said something about that last summer," Dan observed, "but what does it mean?"

"It means that you will be free! You can go south to find your Amanda. Or you can continue to work for me. Or you can look for other work without fear of being a slave. You and your people will face new times."

Dan wrinkled up his face in puzzlement not sure what to do with this piece of news. But he did have enough presence of mind to ask, "But is it safe for me to go to town with you now?"

"I think so!" Curtis exclaimed, seeming somewhat nervous despite this assurance.

Dan continued with his chores, musing about the forthcoming trip as well as wondering why Curtis mentioned Amanda if he knew she were dead?

Chapter XI

Confrontation in Biddeford and Saco

In late morning Curtis released Dan to go home and to "get his things together" and "come back quickly." Dan did as he was told, his mind racing about a series of events which he did not understand. And what was to happen to him in the unknown world of the town? What dangers lurked ahead? Could Curtis be trusted to protect him? or was this Curtis's way of getting rid of him? Dan felt his heart pounding hard in his chest.

Together they hitched Red, the best horse on the farm, to the wagon and set out through snow that was six to eight inches deep, much deeper in drifts that had piled up along the open stretches of road. This time Dan rode on the seat of the open wagon, along side Curtis.

Curtis was quiet. He treated the horse fairly decently except when the wheels got caught in the deep snow and Curtis grumbled, "Wish we'd brought the sleigh." Once they almost returned to get it since they both had to get out in waist-deep snow to put their shoulders to the rear wheels to make it through a drift. When Dan got back onto the seat he was shivering so much his teeth shattered. Curtis reached into the back of the wagon and pulled out a blanket that he handed Dan, almost respectfully. Shortly thereafter they hit long stretches of bare ground so pushed on. When they passed Amos's house, Curtis nodded toward it and Dan felt a sinking feeling in his stomach and confusion in his mind, "What was coming?" As they reached the top of the hill overlooking the river, Dan was astounded to see so many ships. But Curtis told him that they sailed in until the river froze, which would be soon now.

"And all those huge red brick buildings?"

"The York, Laconia and Pepperell Mills," Curtis growled. "Nett used to work in that big building just over the river."

"But what's all that noise?"

Curtis looked at Dan with some disgust, for he was no tour guide. But it did dawn on him that Dan had no experience of any of these things so he continued to explain. "The high whining noise is the sound of spindles, the kind that Nett used to tend when she worked at the York. The heavy thump-thump-thump is the sound of looms. It's the flying shuttles which carry the threads back and forth between the long threads. And they go that way night and day. Some break down all the time so men work night and day to keep as many as possible weaving. If they're stopped, they don't earn any money."

Money and manufacturing was something Dan didn't quite understand and he wanted to hear more. Although he kept looking at Curtis in the hope he would explain other things, Curtis clammed up almost as quickly as he'd opened up. Hence Dan began his own comparisons. He thought that the spindle noises sounded like terns, and the thumping of the looms sounded like rocks he'd heard pounding in a hole out on Bayberry Point. He could not get over the beauty of the ships and river. By this time Curtis had commanded, "Climb back to the tailboard of the wagon so nobody can creep up from behind and rob us."

Dan didn't see anybody about to leap on their tailboard, but he complied, figuring that Curtis really didn't want to be seen riding on the same seat with a black man. As they drove along Main Street in Biddeford, Dan saw lots of people staring at him. When they reached the grain store near the railroad tracks, Curtis told him to eat his lunch and watch from the back of the wagon. As it turned out, he was alone with the horse and wagon for what seemed like forever. By the way Curtis greeted the storekeeper, he figured they were friends and ate their lunch together. He did not feel comfortable sitting there in front of the store seeing men and boys stare at him. More frightening than the people staring at him was the roar of a locomotive crossing Main Street. The noise from engine and whistle seemed to crush his ears. He'd never seen a train before, nor could he ask anybody about it. It all happened so quickly!

Nor did he quite know what to do when he had to piss, so he held it, hoping Curtis would soon return. He was almost exploding when Curtis got back. Asking where he could go, Curtis directed him to the back of the building and was sitting on the wagon seat when he returned.

Dan hopped on the tailboard and heard Curtis say to the grainstore keeper, "Paul, I'll be back tomorrow afternoon to pick up the bags. Keep your legs together."

The men laughed raucously and waved to one another.

Dan didn't know what to make of their last remark, but he gathered that they would stay at least overnight. Then he wondered where they would sleep.

But much as some of these questions might nag him, he was more interested to look while he could. And perhaps Curtis would tell him more?

They drove back down Main Street to the Post Office where Curtis, once again, instructed him to stay with the horse. Dan obeyed. But only a few minutes had passed before several youths gathered around the wagon. Two adults, too, having just been into the Post Office. So their hands were full of mail, held against heavy brown coats. One had a uniform something like Ralph's so Dan figured he must have been in the war. Dan felt like running, for he didn't like to be stared at. Before long, one of the young men began to taunt Dan, screaming, "Blackie, blackie, blackie! Nigger, Nigger!" Others joined in, and the chant filled the street. It was horrifying to Dan. But he said nothing, figuring Curtis would soon hear it and come to his rescue. After all, Curtis was depending upon him to stick with the wagon and horse.

Time crept by, Dan held his position and the reins of the horse and the chant continued. One youth picked up some snow, pressed it together with his hands, then let fly. Others followed. By this time a town constable had arrived on the scene to see what was happening. When he assessed the situation, he shoo-ed the rabble rousers away, turning to ask Dan, "What are you doing here?" Dan explained that his "owner," Mr. Curtis, was in the Post Office and he was tending the wagon. This quieted the constable who proceeded to pace the side of the street nervously, looking from Dan to the Post Office door and back to Dan repeatedly.

Finally Curtis showed up, with his usual armful of mail. "Oh, hello constable," he said, almost jauntily. "What's wrong?"

"Look, John, you better get this nigger out of here. He's just caused a riot here on the Main Street. You know he doesn't belong here."

"But, Dick, I told you that I had a black hired man and that we were coming to town this week. Isn't it your job to keep the peace?"

"Yes, but I can't help it when the town ruffians show up to show me up!"

"Oh, I see, Dan didn't cause the riot, your young people did! Isn't that YOUR problem, not mine?"

"Let's not get too smart, John, your rights could be your wrongs if you insist upon bringing that damn nigger to town against the advice you have had not to!"

"Maybe,"Curtis responded, noncommittally. "Anyway, we're moving along, going to Saco for a meeting of the Scientists. They WANT to see Dan."

"They're welcome to, but you'd better keep him under cover."

"But haven't you heard that President Lincoln has issued an Emancipation Proclamation to make niggers equal to us beginning next January?"

"Huh!" the constable puffed, "that will NEVER be!"

"We'll see, Dick, we'll see. I'll be back through tomorrow."

They drove off down Dean's Hill toward the covered bridge which would take them over the river.

Dan continued to be in awe over the size of the mill
buildings...and all made of brick, too!

As Curtis drove down the hill, he smelled trouble
brewing in the covered bridge. He had "been there before"
and been subjected to some of the taunting that went
on...in fact had once been pissed on by a boy standing on
the overhead cross beams. Also he had heard of residents
being hit by bags of horse manure thrown down from
above. He knew he'd have to drive pretty fast despite the
slippery conditions of the road to escape the rowdies who
repeatedly harassed the populace. Suddenly he hit upon a
scheme. Perhaps his ship captain friend, Earle Romney,
was in port and could loan him a couple of sailors to
make the run through the bridge. So he turned down
Water Street and along Cleaves, peering over piles of
cargo on the dock to see if he could see the schooner's
masts. Sure enough, Romney's ship was in port and they
were unloading cotton.

Dan was glad for the detour, for it gave him the
opportunity to see more of the Biddeford wharves. He
was astounded to see the stacks of cotton bales. The
sounds also fascinated him, sounds of ropes whipping in
the masts or running through pulleys, the sounds of men
grunting and groaning to get the bales onto the wagons
that would haul them to the mills. The block and tackle
used to take the bales from the holds of the schooner
played their own music as he heard men, working in
rhythm, singing their chants to assure the timing on
pulling the ropes.

As they pulled up to the schooner's side, all eyes
were turned toward Dan. "Hey!" Curtis opened, "Captain
Romney around?"

"Yeah," a huge man, with a bad arm, yelled. "He's aboard in his cabin. But where did you get Rastus?" pointing to Dan.

"He's my farmhand, came up on the underground railroad, good worker."

The men muttered among themselves but continued to work as Curtis stepped down from the wagon, told Dan to stay with the horse, and went aboard the Schooner, "Christian Fairfield."

Dan watched the men work. They were tramping through a kind of black mush, mud and snow mixed together. What they were doing was hard, but they did not heed his watching. Before Curtis returned, however, the large man left his work and walked slowly to the wagon. Speaking in a low tone, he advised, "Better be careful, lots of hostility to niggers in these two towns. Curtis wont protect you unless his own skin's at stake. I've known him a long time. He's a bad one!"

Dan merely nodded and said nothing; the big man's viewpoint certainly coincided with his own but he dared not say anything publicly and give Curtis an excuse to beat him.

"I'm Reed Romney, Earle's brother, spent lots of time in the south juggling cotton bales. Your people work hard down there, and I hope that Lincoln was right in starting a war to free your people. Not fair in a free country to do what we do."

Dan felt like hugging the man to hear him say such things, but he could only say, "Thank you."

Reed turned to his companions and yelled, "See, I told you there were polite niggers around. Did you hear him thank me?"

The men guffawed in unison, but Reed paid no attention to them, looked up just in time to see his brother and Curtis come down the gangplank. Dan almost swallowed his tongue when he saw them followed by a third man whom he knew he'd seen before. It didn't take long to figure it out. Sure enough, it was the man on the horse, the man who had taken something from the two men in a boat when Curtis was away. Dan's mind raced both backward and forward: "What was he doing here? And who was he anyway?"

Curtis and Romney came alongside the wagon, looked at Dan, then Curtis announced in a firm voice, "Earle's gonna loan us Reed and his first mate to get us through the bridge."

Dan said nothing but eyed the mate, and the mate stared back. Dan was quite sure the man had never detected him watching from the bushes yet he could not be sure.

With no further introductions or comments, Curtis climbed up on the wagon seat, said "Giddap," as Reed and the mate mounted the wagon, too, Reed climbed up on the seat with Curtis and the mate sat on the horse's hay in the middle of the cart...a few feet from Dan, still on the tailboard.

When they reached the entrance to the bridge, Curtis stopped the horse and Dan noted that Curtis had plied both men with liquor he was carrying under his seat.

At this time, too, Reed beckoned to his partner and they dismounted from the wagon.

"We'll walk on ahead and scour the little bastards out of the rafters," Reed announced.

And that they did! Bellowing at the top of their lungs as they walked ahead of the wagon, the two men scared the hell out of the same ruffians who had challenged Dan in front of the Post Office. They jumped out in droves. When one tripped and Reed grabbed him by the seat of the pants, he began to cry, screaming, "Don't hit me! Don't hit me!"

Reed snarled at him, picked him up by the scruff of the neck and carried him to the rear of the wagon. Shoving him toward the Biddeford side of the river, he shouted, "Go home, and never let me catch you on this bridge again!" The other boys scampered at full speed toward Factory Island, across the river from the "Christian Fairfield," which Dan and Curtis had just visited. Dan remained calm during the few moments they were in the bridge and was startled by the way all the noises echoed from one end of the bridge to the other.

Once at the foot of York Hill, Curtis stopped the wagon, thanked Reed and the mate for helping, offered them another drink, then said, "Hope those guys got the message and aren't back when we come through tomorrow."

"Sorry, John, can't help you tomorrow, we're weighing anchor against the ev'ning tide. Gotta get out of here before river freezes," Reed declared, matter of factly.

"Thanks anyway," Curtis acknowledged as he reined the horse up the hill. Dan continued to stare at the huge York Mills on his right from where he sat on the tailboard of the wagon. And he continued to marvel at the noise. At the top of the hill, he saw a large group of men waiting near the gate. He worried about what they might do.

Curtis must have sensed Dan's fears, for he shouted back, "It's all right. Those are men from Canada, lined up to apply for a job. The mill is expanding its production and needs more people to work on the machines to make cloth for the war."

Dan observed that they were very quiet and orderly.

As they turned the corner in York Square Dan also noticed huge buildings which he'd never seen before. Curtis must have seen him staring at clothesline between the buildings, for he said, "Boarding houses, where girls like Nett live."

He also began to see signs much as he'd seen in Biddeford. He could not read them, but he could tell from the pictures that the stores sold paint, cloth, grain, and flour. Some, too, had pictures of sleighs and wagons so he assumed that those folk had something to do with...sleighs and wagons! Some pictures on the signs he could not figure out, nor did Curtis respond to his open gaze.

Soon they were crossing the bridge where the railroad tracks went over Cataract Falls. Dan had seen railroad tracks on his trek north and had just seen his first train, but he'd never seen anything like the mist that was rising from the river over the falls. Again, Curtis explained, "The steep drop in the river, more than forty feet, I think, turns the wheels to run the machines in the mills."

Again, Dan didn't fully understand, but he began to feel some gratitude for Curtis's answering questions which he had every time he saw something new. Perhaps he had misjudged Curtis? Yet, Reed's comments about Curtis still rang in his ears.

As they rolled up Main Street, Dan's eyes bulged at the number of stores, the blacksmith shop with its red hot horseshoes and the ringing anvil, the number of wagons and horses squishing through the mud. Never had he seen anything like it! Nor so many people in one place. He also liked the old stone building at the corner of what he later learned was Pepperell Square and was quite sure that the picture of lumber, barrels and furniture meant that they sold those items.

But never had he been the focus of such stares! Everybody on the street turned toward Curtis's wagon. And he knew it was because he was black while all the other faces were white.

After a few minutes he felt Curtis pull the right rein and knew that they were going to turn off. Sure enough Curtis pulled in behind a large brick building. He saw letters on a sign, but he could not read it. As though Curtis had anticipated a question, he said, "This is Saco House, the hotel where we're going to stay. I'm pulling around to the stable. You'll stay with the horses, but I'll look in on you from time to time. There is a kind old stable man who runs the place. You'll be all right if you stay out of sight until I call for you.

Dan was truly frightened to be going into so strange a place, but he knew he had no choice. He could try to run away at his peril.

"Oh yes," Curtis continued almost as an afterthought, "and after supper we are going to a meeting. I want some of my friends to meet you. These are the people who are making a study of everything, the ones I'm showing my notes on geese flying over the farm."

This scared Dan the more. He had heard Curtis mention scientists in Biddeford, but so much had happened he'd almost forgotten. Now, he didn't know what to expect. Once again he gritted his teeth. He figured that this must be the price he had to pay for the opportunity to see the town and such new sights as the York Mills, the river, the thriving wharves, the covered bridge...things he'd never dreamed he'd see in this life or the next!

So Curtis put the reins in Dan's hands, threaded his way between the wagons, and disappeared through the stable's rough-hewn door with long iron hinges that squeaked when it opened and closed. Dan looked around for a place to put the wagon under cover, for it had begun to snow again. Finding a vacant spot in the open shed, he backed the horse and wagon into a place of safety.

"Good thinking, Dan," Curtis said gruffly when he came out of the warm recesses of the stable with a wizened old man at least a foot shorter than Curtis and himself. "Dan, this is Wilbur Francis who will look after you and Red tonight."

Wilbur stuck out his hand to shake Dan's and seemed not to mind that it was black. "This is certainly a first," Dan thought. "Usually I am treated as though I had a disease."

Once these amenities were attended to, Curtis said to Dan, "Mrs. Curtis has packed plenty of food for you. You are in good hands. I'll be back to get you about an hour after dark. Stay at Wilbur's side and you'll be all right."

After Curtis disappeared through the back door of the Saco House, Dan looked down at the old man who beckoned him to secure the horse and bring his bag of food into the stable. But he said nothing, simply went up to the squeaky old door and went through it. Dan followed obediently.

How good it felt to be in out of the cold. Although the air had the heavy smell of horseflesh and manure, at least it was warm! Wilbur led him to a hay mow, pointed to it, then turned quickly on his heel to rejoin the horses.

"What about our horse?" Dan asked.

"I'll bring him in in a moment," Wilbur said in a rather rasping voice.

Dan was so grateful to be under cover and out of the cold and newly falling snow, he immediately sat down in the hay. There wasn't much to see that he didn't already know. The stable was much like the one at the farm, except bigger. The longer he sat in the hay the sleepier he became; it had been a long day and evidently was going to be longer! So in spite of himself, Dan drifted off to sleep.

He didn't know how long he slept, but he awoke with a start, aware of a quick flash from a dream. He was riding up a long hill, bareback, on a mare. He tried to stop her before she leaped into a river, but she kept moving then jumped. He awoke just as the mare was about to hit the water. He felt disoriented, rubbed his eyes with his knuckles, didn't quite know where he was. But he soon heard Wilbur's rasping voice at the other end of the stable and jolted back to his situation.

He then decided he'd better eat the supper Mom Curtis had prepared so as to be ready for Curtis's return. He felt thirsty so asked Wilbur where he could get a drink. Wilbur pointed toward an old iron pump with an extra long handle. Dan had used such a pump only once, but he thought he remembered what to do. He took a dipper hanging near the spout and began pumping the handle up and down. Nothing happened.

"Prime it!" Wilbur exclaimed, then came to show Dan how. Soon water gushed out and he took the full dipper with him back to the stall. He was surprised to see something stir in his food when he got back to it; it was a small rat. This scared him. Would he have to fight rats all night to survive? The warmth he felt for the stable quickly vanished, and he wondered how he would store his food while gone with Curtis? Wilbur heard him drive the rat away and came to his side.

"Don't worry,"he said matter of factly, "they eat well here." They wont bother you 'cause we'll put your food in a tin box down near the door."

This comforted Dan a little, but he didn't relish the thought of having the creatures run across his body in the night. "Maybe I can cover up my head with a blanket from the wagon," he mused.

Chapter XII

Meeting Scientists

True to his word Curtis returned for Dan at the appointed hour, looked him over from head to toe, then said in his usual blunt tone, "Follow me!"

Dan obeyed. They crossed through the open shed where the wagon was stored for the night, crossed an open lane between stable and hotel; Curtis opened the rear door of the hotel, walked in, with Dan close behind.

Dan was almost blinded by the light, but after his eyes got adjusted, he looked around to see the grandest stairway he'd ever seen. There was also a dining room with white table cloths, a bar with men drinking, talking and shouting at one another. He could not understand much of what he saw, but he followed Curtis closely, almost holding onto his coat tails. "So this is a hotel!" he mused. "Where people stay overnight when away from home." He'd heard Curtis refer to this place and others, but had never seen one.

He heard Curtis greet people by their first names so he assumed that the farmer knew them. He also assumed that this is where Curtis came when he was away from the farm for a day or two at a time. He wondered if this is what the Curtises argued about, his staying at a place like this? Also, why the different colored lights, red, blue, yellow? What did they mean? And once he almost coughed up his lungs from the heavy cigar smoke that filled the air. He could see that this coughing disturbed

Curtis, but he couldn't help it. Finally Curtis passed him a cup of water and that stopped the irritation.

For a few minutes they just stood around as Curtis mingled with his friends. When he heard the hall clock strike seven, he saw the men begin to enter a backroom they'd passed in coming from the stable. He went along with Curtis and the group and was very much aware that they were staring at him and not getting too close.

They entered a rather large room. Dan estimated it to be about the size of the main floor of their barn at the farm, with lots of chairs set up in long rows. The men took their seats as they continued to mumble to one another in rather low tones. Dan started to sit down, but Curtis took him by the elbow and escorted him rather firmly to the front of the room where there was a raised platform and several more chairs in a row. Curtis took one of the chairs facing the audience and directed Dan to the one beside him. Two other men joined them on the platform. One of the men had a long white beard and seemed very old; the other had a thick white mustache with eyebrows to match. Both seemed dressed very formally with shiny black coats.

When the room quieted down, the distinguished gentleman with the beard stepped to the podium at the front of the platform and began addressing the fifty or sixty people, all men. He began by saying, "I welcome one and all. For newcomers my name is Dr. Goodwyn Watts, acting President of the York County Scientific and Cultural Society. Members will recall that we are developing our organization from week to week believing that our foundation will be the more solid that way. Tonight is a rare occasion so we are going to dispense with reading of last month's minutes and get right to the program. One of our members, John Curtis, from South Biddeford has brought an unusual specimen with him, one we want to study to increase our knowledge of other peoples. Dr. Harry Lord, our specialist in human species, one very familiar with the works of Charles Darwin, has kindly consented to begin the evening's questions. He is sitting here on the stage with me and John Curtis, so I turn the meeting over to him."

Dan sat almost frozen in his seat. He didn't wholly understand what Watts was saying, but he understood enough to know that something harmful might happen to him. He watched Curtis's face to see if he could discover why the man was doing this to him. Curtis was all smiles and enjoying his place at the center of attention. Dan felt himself getting angry and wanted to run from the room. But he knew that that might destroy him.

Dr. Lord stepped briskly to address the audience, giving a long and complicated (for Dan) speech on Darwin's theory, the evolution of species throughout the world. Then he came to something Dan understood, slavery in the South and the fact that a war was being fought over black people. Again he heard that word, "emancipation," so knew he was the center of focus.

Finally, Dr. Lord concluded his speech, "And tonight we have one of those rare species, an ex-slave from Virginia. A few years ago he came to Biddeford via the underground railroad and he is John Curtis's hired hand. I give you Mr. Curtis."

Dan watched Curtis lift heavily from his chair and walk somewhat awkwardly to the podium; Curtis began, "I am honored to have this opportunity to talk about my man, Dan, who is with us tonight. He came to our farm about five years ago, came to us with his wife, Amanda. Unfortunately, Amanda disappeared somewhat unexpectedly last July and has not been heard of since. But Dan has continued to do good work on my farm. He learns quickly, he is loyal, hard working and gentle. I could not run my farm without him."

Dan thought, "Little does he know how I'd like to kill him, right now!"

Curtis continued. "When I offered to bring Dan to this meeting tonight, I was aware of the Emancipation Proclamation that President Lincoln and his government make effective next month. Also I read in the Maine DEMOCRAT that there are those who regard the Proclamation as 'an unmitigated Abolition Measure.' (I quote from the DEMOCRAT). But still I thought that this was so important an event in the history of our country, President Lincoln's freeing the slaves, that members of this society might like the opportunity to come face-to-face with an ex-slave who is about to get his complete freedom. Dr. Lord has agreed to use his calipers to measure Dan's major dimensions; but before then, I want to ask Dan a few questions then accept questions from the floor so you can have the opportunity to hear from him directly. I am asking Dan to remain seated to make it easier for him to answer your questions."

"First, Dan, do you like living here in Maine?"

Neither Curtis nor anybody else ever asked him that question, but he knew he had to give an answer that Curtis would accept, so he said, simply, "Yes," hesitated a bit, then added, "but it's sometimes too cold!"

At that remark, the men roared with laughter. Dan did not know whether that was good or bad until he heard Curtis say, "We all joke about the weather here, Dan, so you are one of us in that feeling."

"My second question to Dan: Do you like working on my farm and have I treated you fairly?"

Dan was smart enough to know that this answer had to be right, so he quite calmly said, "Yes" even as his heart pounded. As he said it, he had to admit that Curtis had done what he said he would do when the railroad people dumped him at the farm. He simply did not care for Curtis's gruff ways, his beating up animals and threatening people. Nor did he know what Curtis knew about Amanda.

"Now, Dan, tell this scientific society what you do on my farm."

Dan started slowly, "I live in a little house that you provided for Amanda and me. I milk the cows, feed the chickens, help build stonewalls, work on the haying, dig clams, pick berries for the house, haul water for the house and gardens, carry seaweed from the beaches..."

At that point Curtis cut him off and addressed the meeting, "You see, gentlemen, he does what any farm hand might do. At that point a man in the back row of the audience stood up and asked, "But I understand black people are like animals. Does he ever act like an animal?"

At that remark the audience began mumbling to one another, many turning to see who had asked the question.

Curtis stood quietly while the men became silent. He looked out over the audience, holding the podium firmly and responded, "No more than you or I." The men roared with laughter seeing one of their members humiliated like this. Dan sat, stone-faced.

And so the evening passed with Dan under a microscope, question after question until finally Curtis remarked, "Enough of this, gentlemen. Now I am going to ask Dr. Lord to bring his calipers to the stage and measure Dan scientifically."

By this time Dan was not only exhausted but angrier than ever with Curtis, asking himself, "Why did Curtis do this to me in the name of science. Did science do this to everybody? What was Curtis getting out of it? And how did Curtis, a King's Highway farmer, ever fall in with this group of men?"

When Dr. Lord brought his calipers to the stage, Dan winced. "What were they going to do to him?"

Lord, sensing that this might be difficult for both him and Dan, tried to calm him. "This will not hurt you, Dan, we are curious about some relationships. In fact, we'll do the measurements on John Curtis first so that you can see that it doesn't hurt. He sat Curtis in a chair beside Dan and proceeded to measure the distance from the top of Curtis's head to a point under his chin, then announced the measurement, in inches, to Mr. Watts. He then measured the width of Curtis' head, from ear to ear, and dictated the measurement to Dr. Watts, who stood at the podium and relayed the dimensions to the audience.

He then turned to Dan to start the same routine. Dan brushed the calipers aside and stood up as though to protest...at which point the men in the audience "Ah'd and Ooooo'd."

Curtis was on his feet in an instant and commanded Dan with his usual gruff voice, "Sit down!"

Dan hesitated a moment, then cowering, sat down in his chair, squirmed a little, and let Dr. Lord take the measurements. These, too, were relayed to Watts who announced them to the audience.

Lord next asked Curtis to take off his coat and shirt so he could measure his chest and shoulders, repeating the procedure with Dan, much to Dan's visible discomfort. He was so nervous and cold he began to shiver.

When Curtis saw Dan shivering, he put on his own clothes and told Dan to do likewise.

Finally, Curtis went back to the podium and announced, "I want you all to have the opportunity to observe skin pressure so I would ask you to form a line to the left of the stage and each of you come up to shake hands with Dan. Just touch his arm so that you can see what happens to the color of his skin. I will stand by with Dr. Lord to observe or record anything you wish to say."

Dan was furious at the prospects of having to look these men in the face. It was the kind of thing he'd experienced in his dreams because the men in his nightmares were usually white. Too, some of them carried guns, the kind he'd seen coming up on the railroad. But once again he knew he was trapped like an animal, thanks to this scientific trick Curtis had played on him. So he stood up as he was asked to do and faced the

men as they filed up onto the stage. He noticed, too, that
some of the men in the audience remained in their seats,
evidently not wanting to touch him. Some would not
look him in the eye. But when the men actually put out
their hands to shake hands, he found them to be mostly
pleasant. Some had soft hands; others were as hard and as
strong as his own. Nor did any touch his wrist or arm
hard enough to hurt. A few thanked him for being such a
good sport. He was too busy to hear much that they
reported to Dr. Lord, but he felt Curtis's heavy glance.
One man, referred to as Dr. Hale, did say, "Dan's no
different than us." Another called Noyes remarked, "A
very important evening in my life. I'd never seen a
nigger before."

When Dan's ordeal was over and the men regained
their seats, Curtis stepped to the podium to thank them
for their cooperation, then returned to his original seat
beside Doctors Lord and Watts. Watts then stood to close
the meeting, remarking, "This is the first of a series of
meetings we want to hold in order to understand our
fellow creatures. Our library committee is gathering
materials for the membership. Notes from this evening
will be available to all of you as well as those of our
members who couldn't be here tonight. The Saco House
management has agreed to rent one of their small and
newly furnished rooms at a modest cost for housing our
records, local newspapers and other artifacts until we can
have our own quarters. As you will observe, some very
important people in all of York County are joining this
endeavor. It is our intention to incorporate soon as the
York Institute to promote these endeavors.

At that point he turned and nodded to Dan,
acknowledged John Curtis again to say, "We are grateful
to you both for your contributions to science."

At that point he adjourned the meeting and the men began chatting with one another and moving toward the exit of the room.

John Curtis joined a small group of men for a moment or two, then returned to Dan's side. Much to Dan's surprise he said, "Thank you. Now you must go directly back to the stable and stay there. I'm meeting some other people and will see you in the morning."

Dan moved like a shadow through the near-empty room. Men still gathered in small knots eyed him from a distance, but not one person spoke to him as he slipped out through the back hallway, walked across the alley to the stable, noting that the snow had stopped falling.

Chapter XIII
Confusion Going Home

Dan's next few hours were hellish. The rats had not gone away. An old ill horse had stunk up the stable. And he couldn't get comfortable in the hay. Also, he was cold despite extra blankets from the wagon. In addition it had been a long time since he'd eaten and he didn't know where his food bag was; furthermore, Wilbur was nowhere to be seen. "Probably sleeping," thought Dan.

He didn't quite know when he'd finally fallen asleep, but next morning he recalled having several nightmares that had awakened him in cold sweat. He didn't remember all the details of the dreams, but he did have one vivid recollection of being thrown into a deep pit with snakes. Another dream involved fire. But try as he might, he couldn't remember all the pictures in his dreams..

Just after daybreak which he saw through a dirty, cobweb-covered window high in the stable wall, he heard a horse whinnying in the alley between the hotel and the open shed so he guessed somebody was hitching up to leave. He also heard Wilbur's gravely voice so knew that he could now get some food. So he got up, folded his blanket and prepared to leave. Wilbur hobbled along, greeted him, and said, I hear you were a "hit" last night. Dan wasn't quite sure what that meant so scowled a little. Wilbur was astute enough to see Dan's puzzlement, added, "The men of the society liked you." Dan smiled then asked for his food bag. Wilbur fetched it, directed him to the water pump again, and went about his chores.

Dan ate as quickly as he could, then went to tend the horse.

Not long afterward John Curtis staggered out the back door of the hotel and just barely made it to the wagon before collapsing into it.   Dan wasn't sure what to do except pump some cold water for Curtis.   When he held the cup to Curtis's mouth, the farmer violently pushed it aside and swore at him.   Twice more, he tried to make him drink, saying, "Suh, it will be good for you."   But he would have none of it, muttering, "Let's go home...let's go home..."

Finally Curtis took the cup to his lips and drank a little.   Dan could smell liquor on his breath, also he thought he detected the smell of a strong powder or perfume.   "What," he thought, "did Curtis do after the meeting?"

Leaving Curtis for a moment and returning to Wilbur, who seemed to be a forthright fellow, Dan asked, "Do you know what happened?"

Wilbur wondered if he should tell this black man everything he knew, speaking in little spurts, "Liquor...women...red light rooms...debauchery."

Dan understood only vaguely but eventually guessed that there was heavy drinking in the bar last night, celebrating Curtis's success with the group.   Also there seemed to have been at least one woman involved, for Wilbur kept mentioning something he didn't understand about "red light rooms."   Before Dan took leave of Wilbur, the stable master warned him, "Don't tell him I told you anything."

Dan then asked, "What about paying for keeping the horse and wagon?"

Wilbur said, "Don't worry, Curtis comes here frequently, often joins others for wine, women and song; he'll pay the clerk sometime even if he didn't this morning."

Laden with this new information, Dan returned to the wagon where Curtis was still stretched out on the blankets they'd brought with them. His bag was nowhere to be seen, but a few minutes later a young boy came dragging it out the back door of the hotel and together they put it into the back of the wagon.

At that point Dan tried to communicate with Curtis, "What d'ya want me to do, suh?"

Curtis groaned a little, opened his eyes a little, tried to talk coherently, and finally blurted, "Bad food and liquor. Drive me home."

"But what about the grain we were going to fetch?" Dan inquired.

"To hell with it...fetch it next week." Then he continued groaning, burying himself under the blankets.

Dan knew how to drive the team, of course, but wasn't it dangerous for him to be seen driving down Main Street and to Biddeford across the covered bridge? What if those ruffians were there and tried to stop him or beat him up? All of these things were spinning in his mind as he climbed onto the seat, checked to see if Curtis was safely in the wagon.

As he pulled out of the Saco House alley and onto Main Street, he noted that the street was already filled with horses and wagons. The day's activities seemed fully underway. He took it all in with huge gulps of excitement And he hadn't driven more than a half dozen wagon lengths before he heard somebody say, "Hello, Dan."

He looked toward the sidewalk and saw Dr. Lord hustling along in the slush. "You were good last night," Lord applauded, walking up to the side of the wagon.

Dan slowed the horse a little and acknowledged the greeting, continuing toward the railroad bridge. Lord walked along with him and two other men he recognized from the night before also yelled a greeting. One queried, "Is Curtis badly hung over?"

Dan only nodded and kept the wagon moving. Imagine his surprise to hear a locomotive whistle down the track and see men come out on the bridge to stop the wagons. Upon hearing the train blast, Red lurched in the harnesses but did not run so Dan kept control. He watched wide-eyed as the train with lots of cars behind it rumbled across the bridge. And he was surprised to see the steel rails bouncing up and down on the bridge as the cars passed! He wondered why they didn't break and plunge the train into the river.

By the time the train passed several other wagons, heading for Biddeford, had pulled along side. Again he recognized one of the men, the man with the hardest hands he'd ever felt. The man introduced himself as Loring Swett, the village blacksmith. Quite bluntly, he said, "Thank you for last night. I'd never met your kind. You helped me understand our species. But I fear you're in trouble. I can see that you are trying to save Curtis from embarrassment, but do you know about the covered bridge?"

Meanwhile, Curtis continued to groan in the back of the wagon.

"Yes, Mr. Swett. We got help from Captain Romney yesterday. His brother and first mate took us through.

"Did you talk to the mate?" Swett asked, intensely.

Dan said, "No suh."

Well, he was arrested last night for smuggling rifles to the Confederate Army.

"That must be bad?" Dan queried.

"It sure is," Swett observed, loudly, "he could get life imprisonment."

Again, Dan wasn't sure what it all meant, but he aimed to ask Curtis about seeing the man meeting the boat in Curtis Cove. Right now, though, he was concerned for his own safety.

Swett seemed to sense that and said to Dan, almost with a commanding tone, "Look, you follow me through the covered bridge. If any of them ruffians try to hurt you, I'll take care of THEM!"

Dan felt kindly toward the blacksmith, who knew that he needed help. "I might be able to beat off those young louts," Dan mused, "but I don't want to hurt any of them or run into that constable, Dick, again." So he agreed to follow Swett.

Once the train roared through they drove over the bridge, passed several wagons coming from Biddeford, took lots of ugly stares and one cheerful hello, and drove down York Hill onto the covered bridge. Sure enough the troublemakers were in the rafters, urinating on passers by, and shouting obscenities. Swett was a man of his word, however, he shook his fist at them, threatened them and shouted foul threats which might have rattled their ancestors' graves.

Once through the bridge Swett pointed in the direction of the docks, indicating how Dan should go, then disappeared up Dean's Hill with the barest of farewell waves.

Dan had a vague sense of the direction he should go, for he knew that the road home went along the ridge overlooking the river. This took him past the wharves where cotton and cord wood were now stacked in huge piles. Several men were loading wagons. Dan looked back past the covered bridge to get a last view of the mills. He observed, too, that the schooner, "Christian Fairfield," was gone and the river was still clear of ice.

Finally finding the path that Curtis had called The Pool Road, Dan kept the wagon rolling at a steady pace despite patches of snow and ice. Every so often Curtis would groan, roll over or sit part way up on his elbow to ask, "Where are we? Of course, Dan didn't know many landmarks so he could say little more than "on the way home." At one point he indicated more precisely, "Just passing Amos's farm."

Down the road a piece Curtis finally sat up straight, looked up into a sky sporting a lemon yellow sun, and ordered, "Dan, stop!"

So Dan pulled the wagon into a field at the side of the road.

Curtis slowly slid down to the tailboard of the wagon, half fell and half climbed out onto his feet, grabbing his fly. Turning away from Dan, he opened his pants and proceeded to piss into a patch of snow looking at the yellow hole as though in a trance. Then for a moment, sort of in a stupified daze, he looked around as though getting his bearings or trying to figure out where he was, all the while muttering, "Where are we? Where are we? Where are...?" He must have passed two quarts before stopping, shaking his penis, then returning it to his pants but forgetting to close his fly.

For a moment he grabbed the side of the wagon, looked up at Dan, still sitting on the seat, and holding the horse's reins. Sort of slurring his words, he stammered, "Guess I did wrong last night...got drunk...you and I were too successful...and that woman..." He stopped as though hit with an axe, looking up at Dan as though to see whether or not he heard.

Dan said nothing. He had gotten over his fear of getting out of town without trouble. And although he felt a certain pity for Curtis, he was secretly glad that the man had met his match. "Perhaps," he thought, "Curtis might treat others better in the future?"

Curtis crawled slowly back into the wagon, lay back on the blankets again, and Dan gently flapped the reins to start the horse.

All proceeded well until they got to the first sight of the marsh. Dan stopped to give the horse a rest before driving him through sand and muck...a little heavy going.

Again, Curtis woke up, got out of the wagon to relieve himself. A little more sober than at the first stop, he looked up at Dan and said, "Thank you for driving me home, but don't you dare tell Mom Curtis or Nett about anything you saw. I'll tell 'em what I want them to know."

Dan had rarely heard him refer to his wife as "Mom Curtis;" but as he nodded agreement about not talking and looked down at Curtis, he was surprised to see some long yellow hairs shining in the sunlight. They were hairs he'd only seen on women's heads so he figured Curtis might be in trouble. But he didn't know whether or not to mention them for fear of Curtis's flying into a tirade. So, he pretended to see nothing while guessing what might happen when Nett and Mom Curtis saw them.

Chapter XIV

Stormy Receptions

As they pulled past the new barn and along Amanda's Cove, Dan was intensely aware of how much he had come to call this area home. He even felt warm about it. It was early afternoon and the sun was a yellow disc over the marsh. There was a scattering of seagulls flying over the river at high tide. He noted how much more desolate the whole area now seemed than just early in the summer when the days were long and his hopes of spending the rest of his days with Amanda were longer.

When they passed the wooded entrance to the path to Dan's house and turned into the main lane, Dan felt nervous about what they would find at the farm. He certainly didn't look forward to any explosions which might occur over Curtis's "illness" and indulgence in town life. He wondered if he should do anything special to smooth the entrance to the farm situation. And what to do?

These thoughts were passing through his mind when Curtis sat up in the cart, crawled up on the seat beside Dan then took the reins. "You get back into the cart," he ordered. "I've gotta be driving when we reach the house."

Dan complied, fully aware of what Curtis was trying to do to cover up. He also knew that Curtis needed some more time so would probably insist upon unharnessing the horse.

Sure enough, as they pulled into the yard, there was Nett on the porch, waving at them and yelling to Curtis, "Come quickly! Come quickly!"

Curtis acknowledged her wave, replied, "Gotta put up the horse!"

"Let Dan do it, hurry."

Dan imagined what was happening and mumbled, " Mrs. Curtis may be ill?"

"What did you say?" Curtis screamed.

"Just wondered if Mrs. Curtis is all right?"

Curtis said nothing, started to take the harness off the horse. Dan sort of danced around the edges, doing what he could to stay out of Curtis's way even as he helped.

Curtis was quiet, but he was pretty wobbly on his feet. Shoving the heaviest part of the harness to Dan, he said, matter of factly, "Gotta go see what they want."

Not long afterward, while Dan was biding his time, Nett came out to the barn, said, "John Curtis is in deep trouble. Mom Curtis was very sick last night, vomited blood, and can tell that he's been drunk. She feared he would do this when he joined his friends in town. She also thinks he has been seeing a woman in Saco. What do you know about it?"

Dan said nothing, little sensing that Nett knew from his silence that what she said was probably true.

"Oh, I know, Nett sympathized, you probably can't say much because of fear.   But you'd better get used to fighting your fears 'cause you're going to need to. Mom Curtis is on the warpath, 'cause she's discovered a lot of things the last couple of days."

At that point, Curtis appeared at the door of the house and screamed, "Nett, come in, come in here right now!"

This left Dan in the dark, but he didn't like what Nett had said about fear. He was scared, for sure. He pretended to work, but his eyes and ears were on the house. Something awful was happening, as he could tell from the shouting among all three of them. Words like "No! You can't do that to me!" and "Help!" All came bouncing across the barnyard despite the horse's whinnying, the hen's clucking and the cows' occasional mooing. Rex, too, set up a howl.

Dan wanted to "get out of there" and go home, but he thought he'd best go about doing his chores as though nothing were happening. So he fed the hens, began milking the cows.

As the sun began to sink into the oak forest across the marsh, he saw Curtis storm through the kitchen door, his wife, in her nightclothes, right behind him, hitting him with a stick. She didn't follow far, but far enough to give him a loud "Whack!" as he hit the top of the porch steps. As she hit him, she screamed, "Don't you ever come home here again with whiskey on your breath and hair all over you!" Curtis lost his footing on the steps and sprawled forward on the path to the barn.

Dan shrugged to himself and wondered if he should have warned Curtis. The farmer, seeming much older and with shoulders drooped, dragged himself into the barn, saw Dan milking a cow, then slumped into a pile of hay in the mow. Looking up to catch Dan's eye, he bellowed, "You knew I was drunk but did you see any hair on me?"

Dan knew that lying was his only safeguard so he said, "No, suh!"

Curtis muttered, "Blind nigger, blind nigger, blind nig...," then slumped over in the hay.

Dan did not know what to do next except continue with the cows. So he finished stripping one and began milking another...making as much noise as he dared. He slowly finished all of them and put the pails away. He then went over to Curtis and calmly announced, "I'm going home for the night. See you tomorrow."

Curtis grumbled a little from his bed in the hay but voiced no objection, so Dan set out down the bushy path to his little house, wondering what might happen next. Little did he anticipate the surprise encounter which awaited him.

****

As he slogged up the hill through the fluffy snow and observed that Amanda's grave, to his left, was fully obscured, he sensed that something was wrong. He stopped, looked around, noted rabbit and deer tracks, felt snowflakes blowing onto his face from the one evergreen overhead, and noted too that the breeze had picked up. It was not pitch black, but he thought he saw a tiny point of

light coming through a crack in his cabin. It was not until
he walked around in front of his house and started up the
porch that he saw a stranger's footsteps and knew
something wrong.   By this time it was too late to turn
back, for he saw his door open gradually, then looked
straight down the barrel of a gun. Dan froze. Nor could
he quite see who was holding the gun.

"Come in here, you nigger bastard," a voice cried in
a loud whisper. "And don't say a word until I tell you to."

Dan did as he was told but began to shiver. Within
seconds he was not only staring into the gun but also into
the face of the first mate of the "Christian Fairfield."
"But," Dan reasoned, "I was told he had been arrested last
nite. He must have escaped."

"No false moves," the man said, as he observed
that Dan recognized him.

"Look, you son of a bitch, I wont hurt you if you do
as you are told. If you don't do that, then I'll put a bullet
in your head."

Dan said nothing, continued to shiver as he froze
into a rigid position. Beginning to make his way through
his dilemma, he didn't think the mate would shoot for
fear of being heard by Curtis or Smith. It seemed only
sensible that the mate had surveyed the area and knew
who was around.

The mate broke the strained silence: "Of course,
you know who I am because I saw you at the docks and
bridge just yesterday. They caught me for smuggling
arms. You also saw me some weeks ago, taking money
from the men in the boat; then you saw me ride down the

road. I saw you, too, watching from the bushes. I want
only one thing...food and a hiding spot. They'll be after
me in the morning, at daybreak. I'm staying here until
my buddies in the boat meet me on the beach, at dawn. By
the time the posse gets here, I'll be out to sea with the
'Fairfield.' Do you he-ah me?"

"Yes, suh," Dan responded, nervously.

Again, the hold-up man spoke. "My name is Elmer
Swan and I want respect. I know what you and Curtis did
last night to con those men at the Saco House. You're not
gonna do that to me."

Dan said nothing, well aware that he was still
looking at the bad end of the gun.

Elmer saw Dan's staring at his gun, then said,
slowly and firmly, "Yes, and it's loaded. But I'm going to
put it down, within reach, while you cook me a hot
supper."

Dan reviewed in his mind what he had in the
house, some bacon, a few potatoes, some corn bread, and a
little milk. So without further exchange with Elmer, he
built a fire in the stove and started to cook supper. Elmer
watched him with squinting eyes. Though he'd lighted
the lamp, it was still pretty dark in the cabin. Then he
asked, "Is there anybody likely to drop in on you tonight?"

Dan said, "No, suh," but secretly wished that
somebody would come by to rescue him. He wasted little
motion in cooking the bacon and potatoes while warming
up the corn bread. Soon delicious smells filled the small
room. Having eaten little in two days, Dan was hungry
and his mouth watered.

All went well until Dan noticed that he had no water. He had left the pail empty so it wouldn't freeze when he went off to town. So he said as calmly as he could, "We have no water. Do you wanta go after some or shall I?"

Elmer grabbed his gun, then in a threatening voice shouted, "No tricks. We'll both go."

That was fine with Dan, but he worried a little about getting down hill and back without falling, especially since he was supposed to walk at gunpoint. Gradually they moved out of the house and into line Elmer prodding Dan as he walked down the steps, along the path, and down the hill. Dan went cautiously, for he didn't want to slip, giving the intruder an excuse to shoot him accidentally. He had seen what hunters had done to deer and other wild game and certainly didn't want to suffer that fate.

They got to the well; Dan broke the ice with his heel, dipped the pail into the water and was tempted to throw it in his captor's face. But he quickly abandoned that notion when he felt the gun dig a little deeper into his side. Before he turned around to walk back up the hill, he stole a glance across the marsh and saw Smith's light shining dimly. Slowly he walked back to the cabin, even remarking, "Don't slip; if your gun goes off, Smith and Curtis will hear it."

Elmer snarled, "Don't tell me what to do, nigger. Keep walking and shut up!"

They reached the cabin safely. Dan savored the smells and hoped there would be enough food for him.

He watched as Elmer sat back in his favorite chair and laid the gun across his lap.

"May be he'll go to sleep after he eats," Dan, to himself. But went on to speculate, "But what would I do then? I don't know how to use his gun! Curtis would never teach me to shoot."

Elmer ate as though he'd not had a meal for a week though Dan knew he must have eaten the day before. Dan, too, munched a few bites of bacon and potato...though the bread was short, still it tasted good.

As long as he was doing something, Dan slowly calmed and gradually felt natural. "But what," he thought, "would happen if either he or Elmer went to sleep?" He felt very tired, for he'd not slept too well at the Saco House stable the night before. And Swan must be tired, having walked from town or come on a horse? If he had a horse, where was it?

Elmer must have sensed this questioning, for he broke the brooding silence. "Look," he practically cooed, "My horse is over in the shelter of your new barn. I gotta get her out of there at dawn. I want you to stay awake while I sleep, then wake me up at daybreak. I'll sleep back there on your bed in the dark, but I warn you. I'll hear ev'ry noise and will blast your head off if you try any tricks."

"I don' wanta get killed, Mister Swan," Dan assured him. "You go ta sleep an' I'll keep watch."

So Swan crawled onto Dan's bed in the back corner of the cabin, and Dan moved the lamp so it was even darker. Dan cleaned the table from the supper, then sat down in the chair beside the stove, hoping he might be able to doze a little without disturbing Swan. And doze he did, having another of those dreams in which rocks were tumbling over him like combers on the beach. Also, when he woke, he knew he'd been asleep, for he'd heard gulls diving for fish.

Looking around to see that all was well and hearing Swan snore, he closed his eyes and dozed again. This time he was awakened by a sharp rapping on his door! He was startled. Nobody ever came to his door. "Was it the Biddeford constable or sheriff? Could it be Curtis? Who?"

Before he could respond, he heard Swan whisper through clenched teeth, "You bastard, nigger, you said nobody would come here."

Before either Dan or Swan could move, the pounding began again. This time, Dan could hear Nett's voice, "Dan, Dan, Dan, wake up! Something terrible has happened! You've gotta come out to the house."

Dan turned to Swan and spoke firmly, "Stay still and be quiet. I can handle her."

He picked up the lantern and went to the door, opening it cautiously. There was Nett, hysterical, and holding on to Rex, the old hound, with a short rope. She was dusted with snow, having come through the bushy path. She was also out of breath, evidently having run. The dog, too, was panting and began nosing around the cabin door.

As Nett stepped through the door into the half light, Dan could not help notice how beautiful she was, the cold having brought out the red in her cheeks. But he noticed something else. She was wearing a bandana around her head that he could have sworn belonged to Amanda. But everything happened so quickly and in a blur that he overcame his shock at seeing it and asked Nett to come in out of the freezing weather.

Without further discussion or warning, Nett repeated what she had said while pounding on the door, blurting, "Dan, you've got to come quick. Curtis got drunk again. Came back to the house and beat up Mom Curtis something terrible. She may be dead. And Curtis is back in the barn, drunk as a coot."

"What started it?" Dan asked, trying to keep his heart from jumping into his throat.

Nett drew a sharp breath, looked away for a moment, then went on. "He came into the house looking for me, found me in my room, then tried to rape me in bed. I screamed. Mrs. Curtis came to the door, thin and exhausted though she was, tried to pull Curtis off, and began screaming at Curtis. Mom Curtis screamed, 'You can't rape her the way you did Amanda. You can't, John, you can't! And you can't throw her off the rocks the way you did Amanda. Get off that girl, and get back to the barn!.'

"Curtis got off my bed and I slipped out the other side, untouched. Curtis turned around, picked up his wife and slammed her against the wall, again and again until she slumped like a pile of rags on the floor, senseless. He picked her up again, carried her into her room and flung her onto her bed, then he clumped down the stairs, went out the kitchen door, slammed it behind him. I looked out the window to see him stagger into the barn. I tried to

stir Mom Curtis but couldn't, got dressed, and came here
for help.

"Truly," Nett continued, almost breathless and
beginning to cry, "I think he's killed her. Come quick and
help me. We may all be in big trouble."

Dan was puzzled. What could he do, with Nett
pulling him one way and Swan lying there on the bed
with a gun aimed at his head? What was his next step?

Trying to slow his own heartbeat, he took a deep
breath and looked into Nett's eyes. "I promise you, I'll
come. Curtis sounds too drunk to harm you now. I've
gotta do something here that will take a few minutes.
Please go back to Mrs. Curtis's side, see what you can do
for her. I'll be right there. Keep Rex with you. I'll be
right there," he repeated, trying to reassure her.

Nett hesitated for a moment, continuing to cry,
then turned; and, with the dog whining and sniffing as
they shuffled through the snow, vanished down the path
to the house.

As Dan closed the door, Swan came off the bed and
into the light. He did not have his gun with him. And he
caught Dan's face in the lamplight, said, "I heard all she
said. You may be in big trouble. I'm in trouble enough
and won't go with you. But I need this hiding place until
dawn. And I still need you to wake me. What can you do
to help?"

Dan was relieved that Swan felt no urge to keep
him there or accompany him to the house. But how
handle the gun smuggler's needs? In fact, for the first
time in his encounter with Swan, he felt in charge. "Ah,"

he thought, "the cellar; it's cold down there, but Swan can wrap in a blanket."

So he nodded to Swan and replied, "I know what you can do. You can crawl down into the cellar. Nobody knows the place exists. Take a blanket with you, also the lamp, but be careful you don't set the floor timber afire."

He quickly pulled the old rug from the trapdoor, lifted it, and showed Swan where he could hide, also assuring him, "I'll be back from the house before daybreak to wake you so you can meet your friends on Curtis Cove beach."

This seemed to quiet Swan; he picked up his gun, and slipped noiselessly into the black hole under the floor. Dan handed him the lamp and a blanket, also instructing, "If you need to get out, just put your shoulder to the trap door."

As Dan put on his outer coat, he heard Swan having a piss down there and imagined he could smell it!

Chapter XV

Deathly Encounters

As Dan started along the bushy path, he felt snow brush onto his face even as the stars seemed to be appearing through the overcast they'd experienced for a couple of days. And he heard an owl hooting far off in the forest beyond Curtis Cove. It told him that the wind had shifted around to the northwest. Curtis had told him that that meant clearing weather. Snow along the path was not too deep since Nett and Rex had more or less ploughed it out on their harrowing journey to see him. As he crossed the King's Highway, he felt underfoot their wagon tracks from yesterday, but his trained feet also told him that other horses had passed and continued toward Curtis Cove. He wondered if they had begun to look for Swan. His mind teamed with other questions: "Did Nett have Amanda's bandana? Where had it been? How had Curtis kept his dastardly killing of Amanda so quiet? Did that explain why he had never called in the Biddeford constable whom he'd heard Curtis call 'Dick'? And how did Mom Curtis know? Would he ever find out if she were to die? How could he confront Curtis with this knowledge? Maybe he should kill the man for what he'd done to his wife and life? And who would now tell the authorities? And whose word would stand up against his and Nett's?"

His mind was still tumbling these questions over and over as he approached the barn. He could think only of the churning sea and Amanda's body in it. But he knew that he had to remain alert to the problems at hand. Angry as he was becoming, he didn't have the luxury of thinking too much about Amanda. His own life might be hanging by a narrow thread. He knew that he must first be sure that Curtis was too drunk to walk before he went into the house.

So he chose the longest way around to enter the barn, figuring that if Curtis were waiting for him he'd not be expecting him to come in from the Curtis Cove side.

He was shaking with fear as he lifted the heavy latch carefully to keep the noise down, also opened the door slowly because he knew it sometimes squeaked. But slowly, slowly he opened it enough to slip into the barn and pass through the cow stable, noting that three of them had shit into the trough he'd shoveled out late yesterday. He then passed quietly through the harness stall to a point where he could spy on the hay mow where Curtis was most likely to be sleeping. It was pretty dark, but sure enough there he was, out cold on the hay.

By this time Dan had worked himself into a froth of anger, enough to club the man to death. In fact, he picked up an axe handle and was ready to use it if Curtis as much as stirred. He decided, too, that violence on his part would go against him, unless he had to defend himself from Curtis's blows. And Dan knew Curtis was smart enough to do such a thing with others present. After all, who was going to believe a black man in this hostile territory...no matter how much he might feel at home?

So he tiptoed along the main barn floor, past the wagon and the new sleigh they had readied for use. He tripped for a moment over a bucket of ashes they were saving for the gardens, but recovered his balance, all the while keeping his eyes on the dim form of Curtis there in the hay. By this time Dan had gotten used to the dark so he had less trouble seeing. Furthermore, fear and anger were strong enough to keep him wide awake.

Finally, he slipped through the horse stalls and to the door leading to the house. Again, he was cautious how he opened the door, for it, too, squeaked most of the time. But he got through it successfully and practically ran to the house, his heart pounding harder than ever. At the kitchen door he didn't even pause, but bounced through it, whispering as loud as he dared, "Nett, Nett, Nett, Net..."

She had heard him come through the kitchen door and along the hallway leading to the second floor. So she greeted him at the head of the stairs.

"Am I ever glad to see YOU!" she exclaimed, "Come quickly, quickly!" in a stage whisper.

Dan was uncertain whether or not he should embrace her to comfort her but made a halfway gesture to do so. She began to cry again, but grabbed him by the coat to acknowledge his comfort.

They then turned toward Mom Curtis's room. Nett said, "I can't get a pulse from her, as my mom taught me to do, but I can hear her heart beating feebly."

Dan looked down onto the bed he'd never seen before, onto the patched work quilt, somewhat dim in the lamplight but still recognizable as one he'd seen her making on the porch soon after arriving at the farm. He felt pretty helpless, but he said, "Nett, we have to wake her, get her to talk, so we can find out how she knew Curtis had raped Amanda and thrown her overboard."

Nett nodded, but knew no better than Dan how to do it. Already she had tried cold cloths on Mom Curtis's forehead.

Dan reached down deep in his memory and recalled his daddy using both hot and cold packs on his family's faces. So he proposed doing that. Nett ran down stairs, got boiled water, and brought it back to the bedroom. While they were doing this, Nett talked.

"When I first came here, I sensed Mom Curtis's jealousy and heard them argue two or three times about 'his women in town.' Also, in cleaning out the old closet under the stairs leading to the cupola, I found a dress that I figured must have been Amanda's, covered with blood stains. I didn't know what to do with it, so I rolled it into a small ball and threw it further back under the stairs. It may be there now? I also found the bandana you saw me wearing tonight; it seemed too good to throw away since it was pretty and I'd never seen one like it before."

"Yes," Dan said, "It was Amanda's. She loved it because her mammy had given it to her long ago and it survived our trip from Virginia. She thought it brought her good luck and wore it everywhere."

"Of course, you can have it back," Nett said, trying to steady Dan in his confusion.

"After we wake up Mom Curtis," Dan whispered, almost fearful of the outcome of the night, "let's see if we can find the dress."

Nett nodded, continuing to alternate hot and cold packs.

As they continued their conversation about their life there at the farm, Mrs. Curtis groaned a long low groan which frightened both Dan and Nett. In a few moments, however, the now-crumpled woman opened her eyes and looked around as though she were looking into an abyss.

Nett spoke to her and said, "Mom Curtis, this is Nett, you are safe here, in your own bed."

Dan turned up the wick on the lamp.

The woman did not acknowledge Nett's words but did put out her hand. Nett reached out, too, to hold her hand, kneeling at the side of the bed as she did so. Then, silence...

That lasted for a long time. Nett and Dan exchanged puzzled glances in the deep shadows of the tiny room.

Nett broke the silence, "Are you in any pain?"

The woman nodded but said nothing. As Nett began again, "Dan is also here and your husband is in the barn...," the woman put her fingers up to Nett's lips as though to silence her.

In a few moments, she began in a very low voice, "I'm going to die soon,...but I want to tell Dan how sorry I am...that I've never told him what I knew...about Amanda's death." She spoke very haltingly and they could barely hear her. But Nett and Dan looked at one another knowingly.

Dan finally broke the spell of silence, assuring her, "It's all right, Mom Curtis, why don't you go back to sleep and get some rest?"

The dying woman gently shook her head from side to side. "Now I can tell you...if slowly...what happened...John always had difficulty passing a pretty face...that is why he had two wives before me and lots of prostitutes at the Saco House...but on that night Amanda died...I heard him get out of bed and cross to Amanda's bedroom...you may remember she was to stay here all night because I was sick...I heard him jump on her bed...heard her shriek and scream and fight and holler, 'Dan! Dan! Dan!' then moan into an ocean of tears as John Curtis raped her...he must have hit her with a blunt object...she stopped moaning...and for a long time I lay here wondering what to do next...then I heard John pick her up...heard her in what I thought was a death moan... and carry her downstairs and open the front door...I dared then to get up and look out the window...I couldn't see much...the night was dark and the cove very calm but dark...but in a few moments I heard a mighty splash beyond the cliff overhanging Curtis Cove so I figured he'd dumped her body into the cove...I don't know if she was dead then or drowned later...but I know he raped her and killed her...strong as she was, she was not strong enough to fight back..." At that point Mom Curtis let out a long groan and a gasp, almost in the kind of death rattle Dan had heard his daddy make on his death bed. And he shuddered at the memory.

Waiting a short moment Nett then asked, "Mrs. Curtis, what happened next?"

Mom Curtis turned to look up at them, clearly exhausted and seemingly talked out. But she turned back to stare at the ceiling for a few moments where the shadow from the rim of the lamp etched a circle in the white plaster. Again, she spoke haltingly, "John pounded up the stairs, got back into bed, then muttered, 'Damned nigger bitch, attacking me like that. I fixed her good.' He went back to sleep....but I laid awake until dawn...laid awake many nights imagining the scene...couldn't sleep...had to go to the doctor...Dan, you know that trip...so when I heard him attack you, Nett, I went to pieces...I'd had enough to make me sick for months...I didn't think I could stop him, but I tried..."

As the dying woman uttered these last words, Nett squeezed her hand, but she went into her death rattle again. At that very moment Nett and Dan heard the kitchen door open and Curtis stagger in, uttering his drunken curses.

"It's Curtis!" Nett squealed and grabbed at Dan.

"I'll fix him," Dan assured her, "you stay here."

When he went out into the upstairs hall, he saw Curtis trying to climb the stairs, muttering all the while in a thick drunken voice, "God-damn Nett, God-damn Amanda, - bitch wife....god-damn Dan...he saw that hair...god--damn nigger...god---damn everything!"

Dan saw that he wasn't climbing very fast so had time to figure out what to do next. So he waited as Curtis made one step at a time and continued to swear and curse and flail his arms and shoulders about from stair rail to wall and back again. Dan quickly saw what to do. When Curtis reached next to the top stair, spied Dan, he went wild and reached out to grab him. But by now Dan was so angry and so alert, he timed a push perfectly that sent Curtis sprawling right back down the stairs. He tumbled and rolled like a rag doll and smashed into the wall opposite the bottom step. He lay there as though killed. Dan rushed down to see what he had done, found Curtis

unconscious but still alive. Without hesitation he went
to the barn, got a coil of rope he sometimes used to corral
the horse, returned to the house and tied Curtis, hand,
foot, body, in every direction.

Looking up the stairs toward Nett, he vowed,
"When he wakes up, he'll never move!"

When Dan got back to Mom Curtis's bedroom, he
found Nett sobbing and lying across the extra pillow
beside Mrs. Curtis. He laid his hand on her shoulder, and
she resumed an upright kneeling position.

"She's gone, Dan...no heartbeat...Curtis killed her,"
all this through sporadic sobbing.

Dan said nothing for awhile, then pulled Nett to
her feet. "You can't go on like this," Dan said, matter of
factly. "We have lots to do before the night is over."

He then told of Swan's holding a gun on him when
she knocked at his cabin door.

She greeted this information with a few shocked
"Oh's!" then asked, "What do we do now?"

"I've gotta do as I agreed, go back to wake Swan or
risk getting shot."

"But isn't that helping an outlaw escape?"   Nett
asked.

" Maybe. I don't know much about such things,"
Dan responded, "but we can't risk having him come out
here to see all of this! He has a meeting at dawn with his
schooner mates from the 'Christian Fairfield,' so for now
we've gotta let him get away from here. He thinks a posse
will come looking for him tomorrow. When they come,
we'll get them out here so they can see what happened."

Nett gasped when Dan mentioned the boat and
under her breath said, "My father has shipped lumber and
ice on that schooner!"

She reflected for another moment, then observed, "I guess you're right, Dan. But am I safe here with Curtis while you go wake up Swan?"

"I think so," Dan calmly replied, "come look at him."

So, together they pulled the blanket over Mrs. Curtis's face, walked down the stairs to see Curtis laid out in the hallway looking more like a full capstan than a human being. He was not moving a muscle.

Dan turned toward Nett and said, "If you want to wait for me in the barn, come on out and I'll find a club you can use on him if he gets free. But I don't think he's going to get untied. And Swan mustn't see you."

So Nett put on her coat again, quietly handed Amanda's bandana to Dan, and went to the barn with him. There he found another axe handle for her to use if Curtis somehow managed to get free. Dan was pretty sure that Curtis had enough alcohol in him to last another few hours.

"I'll be back at dawn then we'll go up in the barn cupola to watch Swan meet the dory from the 'Fairfield.' Then we'll look for the posse."

Again, as Dan started down the lane, he was filled with questions. "How could they prove that Curtis killed his wife? Would they find the crumpled dress when they needed it, or had Curtis thrown it overboard, too?" And as he thought about Curtis' raping Amanda, he got the angrier, almost wishing that he had clubbed Curtis to death on those stairs. And "poor Amanda," he muttered to himself, "asleep under that pile of rocks all because of that cruel old man. And to think that Curtis had tried to deceive him or throw him off the track all these weeks when he knew she was dead and hoped the ocean had washed his crime away! He was secretly glad though that he'd kept his silence about finding Amanda and burying her."

When he reached the King's Highway, he could see that more horses had gone at a pretty fast pace toward Curtis Cove. Probably he and Nett didn't hear them because they were dealing with Curtis. Hence, he rushed quickly along the piece of road which might expose him, then dodged quickly through the entrance where the snow had bent the branches as though to form a gate. He bent the branches back to cover his tracks, then rushed up the hill to his home. Stamping his feet hard as he hit the porch, he banged his way into the cabin, hoping this would wake up Swan so he'd not have to call him by name. Sure enough the pounding woke up Swan who hollered up from the cellar, "That you, Dan?"

Dan responded politely, "Yes, Mr. Swan, time to get up."

In a few moments, Swan, shivering even with a blanket around his shoulders, crawled up through the trapdoor, dragging his gun behind him.

Dan pretended to putter around in his kitchen, got a drink of water, watched Swan out of the corner of his eye and handed the outlaw a piece of cornbread he'd hidden for himself the night before.

Swan took the morsel and gobbled it down with a gulp of water, then prepared to leave quickly, not speaking but giving Dan a nod. "Be seeing you," he snapped as he went through the door, stomped down the steps, and vanished into the dawn.

Dan bided his time, took another drink of water, spent a few moments putting the trapdoor back in place and covering it with his rug. He then slipped out the door noiselessly, walked down the path to the King's Highway. This time he waited behind a small evergreen near the entrance because he knew that Swan had to go past that point in getting from the new barn to Curtis Cove Beach. Sure enough, in a few moments Swan galloped past at a high speed. Dan then left his hiding place, and went swiftly across the Highway so as not to be seen, disappearing into a very snowy and unused path. But it seemed better to get wet than risk meeting the posse.

Running every step of the way, he was soon entering the barn where he found Nett sitting on a keg in Red's stall, holding her axe handle in readiness should she need to use it on Curtis. Dan whispered loudly so as not to frighten her, joined her near the keg, then asked, "Any sign of Curtis's waking up?"

"No," Nett said, shivering as she talked even though it was fairly warm there with the horses.

"Quick," Dan ordered, somewhat curtly, "we've gotta climb up into the cupola quickly. Swan has gone to join his friends on Curtis Cove Beach."

So they climbed the ladder, Dan leading, 'til they reached the lookout and squeezed into it. The morning was spectacular. The eastern sky was yellow, tinting the grey ocean surface. They could see the steady revolving lights in the lighthouses of Biddeford Pool and Cape Porpoise. Nett also pointed out Boone Island Light, one Dan had seen before but did not know its name. Crows began to caw in the nearby pine forest across the King's Highway. Dan wished they didn't have "this mess" on their hands so they could enjoy it the more.

By the time they got oriented sure enough there was the figure of a man on the far beach, leaving his horse and walking toward the water, then at low tide. Looking toward the mouth of the cove, they saw a dory moving smoothly along the Timber Point shore; two men were rowing and a third was in the bow, signaling.

Chapter XVI

All Hell Breaks Loose

Somehow the timing was perfect. The men in the boat were meeting Swan at the appointed hour. Nett whispered in Dan's ear, "This certainly took careful planning."

Dan nodded, "They go by sun and tides."

Then they both exclaimed, "Look!" and pointed almost simultaneously.

They saw men on horses riding at full speed from Timber Point along the causeway between Curtis Cove Beach and Little River; they were riding toward Swan.

But Swan didn't see them, nor did the men in the boat. The men on horseback had been hiding behind bushes and boulders along the shore. Dan explained to Nett, "I knew the horses were out there somewhere, with all those tracks in the road. I didn't have time to tell you much about them."

As the boatsmen got closer to the beach, they stood up in the dory and began waving their arms wildly, trying to warn Swan by pointing to the galloping horses. Dan and Nett saw Swan look back then run for his horse. Meanwhile, the boatsmen turned around quickly and began rowing at top speed back toward the mouth of the cove. Swan reached his horse, climbed on and began riding along the beach away from the posse. But then Dan and Nett spied another group of horses riding from the other direction directly at Swan. "It's a trap." Dan said, "the second group must have been hiding in the woods near the end of our lane."

Within seconds they heard a shot fired, saw a member of the second group fall from his horse, wounded; a second shot seemed to hit Swan who dismounted from his steed and tried to climb up the embankment to escape into the pine forest on foot. Quickly the posse surrounded him, sent shots toward the boat. Two riders galloped back onto Timber Point disappearing into the trees at first then coming out on the boulders forming the shoulder of the peninsula...but only after the dory had gotten clear of the cove mouth. One of the two men took out a spy glass and scanned the horizon, evidently looking for the schooner. From their vantage point Dan and Nett could see it lying on the Cape Porpoise side of Timber Island, well out of sight of the two men and ready to rendezvous with the three boatmen.

In a few moments the whole scene was empty of humans, and Nett and Dan climbed down from the cupola to resume their own drama!

"We gotta be careful," Dan warned, "Curtis may have gotten loose and we don't want him to surprise us. He has a gun in the house and will use it on us if he can." From the cupola they had watched the kitchen door but couldn't see the front porch.

Slowly, cautiously, they crept back through the horses' stalls, carefully opened the kitchen side door in the barn. Dan warned Nett to keep her axe-handle club in readiness while he crossed the open space between barn and house. He carefully pushed the kitchen door ajar so he could see where he had left Curtis. As he feared, Curtis was not there.   This sent a rush of anger through Dan's body.   What to do now?   No doubt Curtis saw Nett and him in the cupola and crept out when they weren't looking.   But where was he?   Not wishing to expose himself in the open spaces of the barnyard and hence give Curtis a clear shot, he hugged the house and crept around to peek into the windows.   No Curtis.   This took several minutes.   As he was about to rush the front door, he heard the horse stall door slam, then heard Nett shriek. What to do now?

Again fearing that Curtis would turn a gun on him, Dan ducked around some boulders in the lawn, then made a dash for the cove side door.   By the time he got into the barn, he heard Nett screaming louder than ever but also heard Curtis yell at her, "Don't bite me, you bitch! You're my trouble!"

Dan knew just where they were...in the lower hay mow where Curtis slept after his drunk.

Curtis continued to yell at her while obviously trying to hold her down.   All of this made Dan the angrier, and he hoped that Nett could hold out until he reached her side.

Using the sleigh parked in the middle of the barn floor as a screen, he could see that Curtis had her on her back with his gun across her chest as he fumbled with her clothing and his fly.   Nett continued to scream, kick and bite so Curtis was not having an easy way with her.   But he was so busy trying to rape her that he seemed not to pay attention to where Dan was.

Holding his axe handle firmly, Dan leapt across the barn floor as quickly and quietly as a cat, lifted his club and brought it down hard across Curtis' shoulder. He heard something crack so he knew he's struck home. Also, in pulling up away from Nett, Curtis hit the trigger of his gun and it went off right across her chest, the bullet making a thudding sound as it hit one of the huge timbers holding up the barn. Nett screamed, scurried in the hay and tried to straighten out her clothing to cover her bare flesh.

Dan watched Curtis try to get up, reach for his gun. He was also cursing Dan like never before, calling him every kind of "black nigger bastard" he could lay his tongue on. But Dan didn't yield an inch. While Curtis was off balance, he struck another blow between the neck and shoulders, heard him groan and try to fight back, then fall on his back.

Nett yelled, "Stop, Dan, stop, he's hurt enough, stop!"

Dan sort of regained his senses just as he felt a pair of arms around his chest.

Within moments Nett regained her feet and composure; Curtis keeled over unconscious; and the man holding Dan released his grip. A second man joined them only seconds later.

The taller of the two men finally said, "I'm Sheriff Oscar Palmer and this is my deputy, Jack Fogg. We're here because our prisoner, Elmer Swan, said that somebody might have been murdered out here. We got him out to the new barn before he told us or we'd have been here before. Jack and I have just witnessed this whole scene and thank you, Dan, for what you did to save Nett from a horrible experience. Yes, I know your names because

we've had our eye on this place for months. We knew
Swan was dealing in arms down here somewhere. Also
we understand that you harbored Swan last night, Dan.
That's a crime you know, maybe not where you came
from but it is here in Maine. But things may go easy for
you because of what you just did. We'll have to take you
both to town and probably hold you in jail until we sort
things out.

Nett then asked, "Do you know my father, Henry
Scamman?"

"Yes, Ma'am, we do, a fine man and we aim to tell
him what's happened."

Palmer then went on to ask, "Is it true that Curtis
beat up his wife last night?"

Nett responded, "Yes, he killed her early this
morning."

"Where is she?"

"Upstairs in the house, in her bed."

"Probably it's best that you don't give me many
details now. There will be time for that later. But,"
Palmer continued, turning to his deputy and giving him
an order, "You stay here with these two people and I'll go
investigate."

With that, he turned on his heel and left the barn.
Nett and Dan merely looked at one another. Dan, still
shaky after his attacking Curtis, said in a low voice, but
one which Fogg could certainly hear, "I'm glad they came
when they came. We could have been killed."

"Yes, or you could have killed Curtis you were so mad at him for killing Amanda," Nett observed.

Dan nodded, then stole a peek at Curtis, still lying on the barn floor. None of them seemed to feel any urge to assist the farmer with his injuries, but they could see that the deputy was watching him carefully.

While they stood around waiting for Palmer to return, Dan heard seagulls screaming overhead. He knew one of them had a crab or a fish that another wanted. He also heard one of the gulls plunk down on the roof, a ritual he had observed many times during his time at the farm. He also knew that milking time was long past, and that should be taken care of before they went to town with the sheriff.

When Palmer came back, he nodded his head and said, "Mrs. Curtis is dead all right. Every bone in her body seems broken."

Nett responded, "They are. Mr. Curtis shook her up, slammed her against a wall then onto her bed. But she talked with us before she died. She told us that Curtis also killed Dan's wife, Amanda, last summer."

Palmer seemed appalled by this new news. He stroked his chin and pondered a moment then remarked, "Funny thing, Curtis has a reputation for being a good farmer. Prominent men in Saco know he's interested in science and scientific farming. But they also add something about 'wine, women and song.' Maybe that's the explanation. I also know, Dan, that he took you to Saco to appear before the scientific society and that it was a good session. But enough of this. We have to go to town, get the coroner.

"But, suh, what are we going to do about the barnyard chores, like feeding the animals and milking the cows?"

Palmer turned to Nett and asked, "Can you do it?"

She nodded with a smile.

"Then, Dan, you hitch up the sleigh; we'll load Curtis into the back of that. Nett, you stay here with Mrs. Curtis's body and do the chores. We'll be back this afternoon, with the coroner and the town counsel to get more details. Jack and I will go along with your sleigh in case Curtis gets any more funny ideas. We need to get him to a doctor, too. And, Nett, let nobody into either house or barn. We want no outsider messing up the evidence."

They spent the next half hour carrying out Palmer's instructions, taking off for town just an hour or so after sun-up. Dan knew that from the way the tree shadows fell west.

The trip to town was marked by two events. Going across the end of the marsh, they met Farmer Smith supposedly "out for his constitution," as he put it. When he saw the two men on horseback and Dan driving the team, he queried, "Where's Curtis?"

"In the sleigh. He's been hurt," Palmer explained.

Smith countered, "Was he involved in Swan's capture in Curtis Cove?"

"How'd you know about that?" Palmer asked.

"Met Swan and your men over past the new barn at the end of the road," he replied, matter-of-factly.

Palmer and Fogg said nothing but observed that Smith was curious enough to try to get a look at Curtis under the blankets in the rear of the sleigh.

"Come on, Dan, giddy up," Palmer ordered.

As they started to move, Smith fired one more question to Palmer, "What was that shot coming from the barn?"

Palmer answered, "Curtis's gun went off accidentally," but gave no further explanation. He turned, however, to say to Smith, "I wouldn't go near the Curtis farm today if I were you. It might not be good for your health."

That left Smith scratching his head as he sat on his horse staring at the vanishing wagon.

Dan didn't worry, for he knew that Smith rarely came to the farm when Curtis was away. He was afraid of Mom Curtis. She had told him off a few times.

Another event slowed the trip to town. Curtis became conscious; although he was somewhat delirious, he was typically abusive.

"God-damn bitch...refusing my pecker...my gun, where is it? God-damn Dan hitting me like that...after all I've done for him...pushing me down the stairs...ropes, ropes, where are the ropes...those cute bastards in the cupola....horses, who fed the horses this morning? what's happening? where am I? shoulders hurt, bones broken..."

Every word made sense to Dan, sitting in the driver's seat, but Palmer and Fogg made the mistake of trying to talk with him, asking him to "say it again."

But it was almost as though he were drunk. He got angrier and more delirious, groaned a lot, complained of pain.

This happened a couple more times during the trip but did not slow the sleigh. Actually, it was the bare places in the road and the detours through the fields that took the time.

As they rode along, Dan went into one of his musing moods. "What would the outcome be of all this? Would he have to stay in jail? And what would happen to Curtis? to Nett? to his job? And what about Christmas? So much had occurred he'd almost forgotten that it was next week?"

Yet, as he rode along atop the heavy farm sleigh he enjoyed the sun on the snow-laden evergreens and snow stuck high on the upper branches of the maples. He felt good, too, about noticing that lots of horses had passed along the road...probably Swan and his men, he thought. And when he passed Amos's place, he noticed that another section of the barn roof had caved in and the barn was full of snow. He also began to have a few fears related to his last visit to town. "Would the ruffians he met at the Biddeford Post Office and in the covered bridge still harass him? How much protection would he get from Sheriffs Palmer and Fogg? How much would being black hurt?"

Dan didn't know how long he had been in this musing state, but he suddenly awoke to the fact that Fogg was speaking directly to him, asking questions about living with Curtis, how it felt to be at the scientific meeting, did Henry Scamman visit very often? Dan didn't know if it helped to answer the questions, but being practical, too, he answered each as honestly as he knew how.

When they reached the wharf section of town, Palmer drove his horse to the front of the team and took over again, directing Dan to drive up Dean's Hill to the center of Biddeford. At the constable's office he got off his horse, leaving Fogg to guard Curtis. Before long Palmer came out, with Dick Adams, the constable, and altogether they removed Curtis from the back of the sled and took him into the building. Once inside, Palmer and the constable shared giving directions.

Palmer began, "Dick, take Curtis in there where a doctor can fix him up. Dan, you stay out here 'cause you're going back to the farm this afternoon. Jack, you guard Curtis."

"Constable, I want the town counsel and the coroner and one of your deputies to go back to the farm with Dan. We've lots of questions to ask. Also, we need to know where the trials are going to be held, so you work on that. If Dan is going onto the stand to testify, we'd better try to get the trial moved from Alfred to Saco.

This piece of information was good news to Dan, 'cause he seemed to have made a hit with some prominent Saco men. Although he did not understand all that was happening, he did understand that. He also knew that he was hungry!

Before too long one of the constable's clerks came in with some bread, ham and drink. Dan attacked his share as though he hadn't eaten in a week. In fact, he'd had very little for several days. Palmer, seeing him eat so heartily, said, "You've done enough work for ten men today. Eat up."

Dan smiled. He sorta liked Palmer as a man, but he also liked the fact that Palmer had seen him slug Curtis and knew why.

Before the afternoon was an hour old Dan found himself driving Red to the grain store upon instructions from Palmer, loading several bags, then returning to the constable's office. Soon after, he was driving back to the farm, accompanied by the coroner and the town lawyer who rode in another and lighter sleigh. He also had clear instructions from Palmer.

"Don't talk with Smith or others about what's happened. They'll find out soon enough. And don't you or Nett leave the farm. Do the chores as you are used to doing them. Don't sleep under the same roof as Nett; in fact, if you think it is safe, stay in your own little house. You are to do only as I say. If I have any written messages, I'll send them to Nett. And if any of Swan's men show up, tell them that I will deal with them. Best that you keep a weather eye for the 'Christian Fairfield,' though I think that now that the river has begun to freeze, it will stay away for the winter."

Dan had listened to the orders carefully; and being the obedient hired man that he had been, he had no difficulty repeating the instructions to himself. His most worrisome questions: "What could happen to him for having buried Amanda secretly? Would they put him in prison for that? And should he tell Nett about it? Would they dig up her body to prove her death?" He mulled over these questions until they got to the edge of the marsh. He then decided he'd better pay attention to guiding the other sleigh through the difficult spots in the road, past the new barn and on to Curtis Farm Lane. And that he did, letting his mind wander only as they passed the little, branch-covered path to his house.

Reaching the barn, Dan got out of the sled, waved to Nett who came running from the house to greet them, then led Red and sled into the barn, leaving enough room for the other horse and sleigh to pull in behind him.

In his own blunt way he said to Nett, "This is Coroner Hayes and Counsel King."

She greeted them graciously and asked if they would like a cup of tea and some biscuits. They assented and she took them into the house. Dan stayed to unharness and feed Red and the visiting horse.

The coroner and counsel were very proper. After eating they went upstairs to see Mrs. Curtis's body. Although she didn't relish the thought of watching the coroner, she asked if she might.

"It's not routine," he responded, "but no harm." In fact, he seemed to welcome her assistance undressing the dead woman even though he looked at Nett curiously when she gasped, "Oh.. oh...oh..." several times. Mrs. Curtis was covered with bruises from head to toe. Already frail from several months of worry and inner mourning, Curtis had really done her in. As the coroner examined her, he made several notes on what looked to Nett like an official form.

When he'd finished and re-covered the body, he asked the counselor to join him and asked Nett what had happened.

She related every detail that she remembered, including the story about Amanda's death. This last piece of information startled the two men because they didn't know there was a second murder involved.

When Nett got to the part about finding Amanda's dress under the stairs, she asked if she could bring Dan from the barn.

They nodded, and she went down to the kitchen door to call him. She yelled many times, but he did not answer. Finally, she ran to the barn to find him fast asleep in the lower hay mow where Curtis attacked her earlier in the day. At first she thought he was dead, but finally she shook him vigorously until he woke up.

"Poor dear," Nett comforted, "You must be exhausted."

Dan sat up, rubbed his eyes to get oriented, shook off a horrible image from a dream then asked, "What is it?"

"You've gotta come in and talk to these men," she insisted. "We've reached the point of finding Amanda's dress."

Still half asleep Dan stood up, began to shiver as he followed Nett, and asked, "Shall I tell them everything?"

"You've got to, Dan, it's the only thing that will keep us out of trouble."

"Or get me into more trouble," Dan muttered under his breath.

"What didja say, Dan?" Nett turned to ask.

"There's lots I've not told you, Nett, but I guess we have to push on."

Nett stopped in her tracks. "I wish you had told me, but there's no time now."

Dan retorted, "Your father and Curtis didn't want me to talk with you, so I didn't. But now we must trust..."

Nett's face turned from fright to bright, and they continued into the house.

Chapter XVII

The Investigation

Just inside the kitchen door, Nett turned and whispered closely into Dan's ear. "I found Amanda's dress."

Dan nodded and they went up the stairs.

Once in the room with the lawyer and coroner, Dan felt very tense.

The lawyer reminded Dan that this was like a deposition and that he must tell the truth.

Dan didn't know what a deposition was, but he did know the truth.

The lawyer then indicated that the coroner had confirmed Mrs. Curtis's death as being caused by internal injuries which presumably came from Curtis's slamming her against the wall. He said it quick and easily, adding, "All of this will be brought into the court when Curtis is tried."

He went on, looking at Dan, to say "Now you must tell us about your wife, what happened to her, what Mrs. Curtis said about it. Tell us all you know."

Dan looked to Nett for encouragement then Dan reviewed each step of their lives together, how they came to the farm, how Amanda did housework, and he helped with the outdoor work.

"Get to the point, Dan," the counsel insisted. "Remember, Hayes and I must go back to town tonight."

So Dan plunged into the details of the night Amanda disappeared, how three days later he discovered her naked and bruised body on the beach near the new barn, how he took her to his house and eventually buried her under the pile of rocks.

As he told the story, he could see that Nett was moved and was crying.

"What didja think happened, Dan?"

"I didn't know whether Mr. Curtis or the ocean had killed her. Although the ocean was calm that night, it got stormy the next day. And Curtis kept talking as if she was comin' back. I only wondered why he didn't call in the sheriff though I don't know nothin' about 'the law'."

"But why didn't you tell Curtis what you knew?" the counsel probed.

"I was scared. I seen him beat up his dog and horse. I heard him and Mom Curtis argue. He was a strong and brutal man. I didn't want him to kill me."

"Did you hate him, Dan?"

"Sometimes when he treat me mean or treat his animals mean. When I saw him try to rape... " At that point he broke down, for he could only think of Amanda.

The counselor paused for a moment, giving Dan time to regain his composure. "All right, go on..."

Dan finished his statement, then paused... "That's why I bashed him with a stick in the barn this morning. I 'fraid he kill Nett and me."

"That's good to know, Dan, but you didn't hate him every day, day after day, and plan to kill him?"

"No suh! " Dan said, emphatically. "We do lots of chores together 'round the farm. He do what he say he do for Amanda and me when we come here...the house, the food, the protection."

"What do you mean, 'protection,' Dan."

"Until I go to Saco to the science meeting, he never force me to leave the farm. He know white folk don't like black folk."

The counselor paused at some length, made some more notes, then pursued a different line of inquiry. "Dan, do you think you would recognize any of your wife's clothing if you saw it?"

"Yes suh!" Dan said, emphatically.

The counselor turned to Nett and asked, "Will you bring out that dress you found under the stairs when you first arrived here?"

Nett got up, left the room, and Dan's eyes followed her. He had been worried about this moment since Nett first mentioned the dress and had handed him Amanda's bandana. In a few moments Nett returned with the dress rolled up in a ball.,

"Open the dress, Nett," the counselor instructed.

At that command, Nett held the dress shoulder high and let it fall naturally to its full length and watched Dan.

He broke into tears and sobbed as if to sob his heart out.

Again, the counselor gave him due consideration and waited, finally saying, "All right, Dan, is that Amanda's dress?"

Dan rubbed his eyes with his fists and nodded. Inside he was in a turmoil. Blood stains were still visible, Amanda's blood. Now he wished he had killed Curtis for what he had done.

The counselor took the dress, folded it carefully and put it in his satchel, remarking, "Dan, we'll use this in our case against Curtis."

"Now, Dan," he said, almost routinely, "we have to discuss your burying Amanda under that pile of rocks without telling anybody."

Dan continued to wipe his eyes, but he knew that he had to stay alert. He still worried about being trapped, yet he kept looking into Nett's eyes for encouragement.

"Could you lead us to the spot where you have buried Amanda?"

Again, Nett looked at Dan with compassion, silently admiring him for his devotion to his wife and marveling how he had survived all of these ordeals. Dan looked at her, feeling that her innocence was on his side. But with no delay, he answered the counselor. "Yes, suh!"

"Would you do it now?"

Dan nodded. And with that gesture, all four of them stood, walked out of the room, put on their coats and walked into the frigid afternoon. Dan noted a hawk kiting over the woods where his home was and wondered if that were a good or bad omen.

They were a motley group slipping and sliding down the farm lane, none of them saying anything, each keeping their own counsel. Dan and Nett, of course, led the way. Snowy though it was, the ground was fairly level. Dan took them to the path covered at the side of the road, indicating that there was usually an opening there but that the snow had bent the bushes to cover it. They walked along the bushy path and up the hill behind his little cabin until they reached the top. Dan pointed to the pile of snow.

"Would you take a few stones off the pile on the side where you buried Amanda?" the counselor asked.

Dan obliged, going to the far side, brushing off some of the snow, then throwing several stones toward the top of the pile.

"And Amanda's body is under there?"

"Yes suh," Dan affirmed.

Both the coroner and the counselor made notes, then the latter asked, "How long do you think it would take to get her body out?"

Dan shuddered, for he wanted her to be there with him always.

"I don't know. Ground's frozen. Could do it in spring, but..."

Nett tapped him on the arm to catch his eye and shook her head.

Dan got the message and said no more.

The Counselor and coroner stepped a few paces aside, whispered something to one another, then returned to Dan and Nett. The counselor began, "What you did was against the law, but we may be able to arrange it so you can leave her body there. Everything else you say seems true, so we have no reason to disbelieve you."

Dan looked at Nett to see her nod slightly.

After they'd made some more notes, the counsel said, "Now, Dan, I want to see where you live and where you hid Amanda and Swan."

Dan now felt very ashamed. He didn't want to show anybody his house. Just as he felt demeaned by Curtis to have his body measured at the science meeting, he didn't like this either. But he knew he must, and Nett confirmed it with a small gesture.

So he led the group up the steps to his tiny porch and on into what by then was a very cold interior. And he'd not picked up since Swan left. He lit the lamp which, of course, revealed the barest of bare interiors...yet a place he and Amanda had come to love. As the other three watched, he went to the back part of the cabin, pulled the rug from the floor, and lifted the trapdoor. He brought the lamp to the edge of the hole, jumped down into the cellar, the floor coming to the level of his chest. He then grabbed the lamp and took it below so that they could all see the black hole. The counsel jumped down with him, leaving the coroner and Nett standing near the cold stove. Dan then pointed to the corner where he had concealed Amanda's body, then said, "I don't know where Swan slept, any place that's flat."

"It doesn't matter," Counselor King observed, "I've seen enough."

They boosted themselves out of the cellar. Dan put the trapdoor back, and they all returned to the farmhouse.

As King and Hayes prepared to part, taking Mrs. Curtis's body with them, King remarked, "You have your instructions from Palmer. You are both to remain here to keep the farm going until you hear from us. We are taking steps to locate Ralph Curtis and get him back here. A trial time and place will be set. You both will be expected to testify. Hard as it may be, you both may have to repeat all of these details again and again and again. Murder is serious business. That may hurt you, Dan, a black slave in white territory unless people take Lincoln's Emancipation Proclamation seriously at the first of the year.

Dan thought, "There's that term again. I hope it means what they say, 'freedom'."

After they had left, Nett began to cry. I must get word to mother and father so they'll not worry if they hear about this.

Dan was in tears himself; and, though feeling awkward doing it, embraced Nett there in the cold barnyard, the sun already a pale disc in the western sky over the marsh.

Chapter XVIII

Surprise Visitors

The next few days went routinely. It was both easy and difficult for them.

Doing the chores was simple enough since they knew the farm routine and were comfortable doing their work. They were attuned to the rhythms of nature, the late rising and early setting of the winter sun on the shortest days of the year. Each kept to their own routine, Nett doing the housework, cooking, cleaning, maintaining the routine which her mother and Mom Curtis had taught her. And Dan knew the chores, too, the care and maintenance of the animals. And they also agreed that it was best that Dan sleep in the barn in case any prowlers were about. They knew that Farmer Smith was both curious and a gossip. Neither had any desire to see him; yet, they agreed that he would probably show up.

Difficult moments included the uncertainty about what might happen next. Smith would be no problem compared with another prison escape by Elmer Swan or even an escape by Curtis himself. They could only hope that both men were locked up tightly and would not return to the Curtis farm.

Some of Nett's uneasy moments came in thinking about Amanda's brutal death, her vivid recollection of Curtis's slamming his wife into the wall; she could hear the deadly thud-thud-thud of her frail body against the wood and plaster and the deadly shotgun blast across her chest. And she could not resist asking Dan about details related to his burying Amanda.   Dan answered her questions about carrying Amanda up the beach to their house. Also he related the story of burying her under the pile of stones. But he didn't mention his feelings, for he knew he would begin to cry...and he believed he should not cry again in front of Nett.

Sure enough, despite the warning that Smith got, he showed up on the second day of Dan's and Nett's running the farm by themselves. Showed up with his beagle, rum on his breath, and pretending to be out hunting. Carried his gun loosely over his forearm.

Dan was in the barn currying the horse when he heard the barn door open and caught Smith out of the corner of his eye. "Anybody home?" Smith asked.

"Yes, suh," Dan responded in his characteristically deferential manner.

"What's this I hear about Curtis being in jail?" Smith queried.

"Don't know much, suh," Dan said.

"Come on now, you know more than you'll say. Are you a coward?"

Dan didn't respond, but he wished somehow he could get word to Nett so that Nett would talk with the man. She knew better than he what to say.   But he remained silent.

Smith paced slowly around the barn, looking the place over to see what he could see. Dan said nothing but kept a wary eye on him.

Fortunately Nett did not come into the barn to give Smith any opportunity to spread scandal. Nor did Smith ask about her. He kept plying questions to Dan, and Dan continued to parry them in the spirit of what Palmer had told him. Finally, Smith said, "All right, you black bastard, stay as mum as you will. I'll ask John Curtis what happened."

Dan did not reply; but as Smith opened the door to leave, he shot a final question over his shoulder, "I hear Ralph Curtis is coming home. Is that true?"

Dan thought for a moment, figured the news would do no harm since it might keep Smith away. "I hear that, too."

Smith paused a moment in the doorway, called his dog, then left as quietly as he had arrived.

Dan breathed more easily when he cracked the door and saw Smith walk down the lane toward the Kings Highway. When Nett handed him his dinner an hour or so later, he told her what had happened, what he had said, and what he thought Smith was up to.

They agreed they should not talk with Smith.

*****

Both of the farm workers were also aware that Christmas was nearly upon them. Nett seemed more upset about their being kept at the farm, for she had gotten permission from Mom Curtis to go home for a few days over the holiday. All Dan had was his memory of his Christmases with Amanda, how they each gave one another little things they had made, a shell bracelet, shell earrings, a comb made from whalebone that had washed up on the beach, a small purse made from pigskin he had salvaged from one of the slaughters. But no more did Dan expect to be giver or receiver.

Both, however, were startled the day after Smith's visit, three days from Christmas. With no announcement Nett's father and brother slid into the yard in a light sleigh. She could hardly contain herself, she was so pleased to see them. Since she was in the kitchen cooking at the time of their arrival, she had no way to prepare for the meeting. They simply walked in on her. Dan was a half mile away, toward Curtis Cove, cutting cord wood.

After Nett had hugged and kissed her father and brother, her father turned to say, "You know, of course, why we are here?"

Nett replied, "I suppose you've heard about Curtis, what he tried to do to me, and how Dan saved my life."

Her father nodded, added that they didn't have many details but that the two murders had scandalized the two towns. He also informed Nett, "And the community is shocked that a black man would save your life."

"But he did!" Nett exclaimed.

"Yes, we know, and it's all right."

Nett went on to give her father more of the details while her brother went to find Dan, Nett sending him in the general direction to discover his location from the sound of sawing and chopping.

When Dan had returned and warmed his hands at the fire, Henry Scamman turned to him and said, "My

family and I thank you for what you did. And we are
sorry about your wife. We knew that Curtis was a drunk
and abused his animals, but we didn't think he would kill
anybody. He covered up pretty well by gaining a
reputation of being a good farmer. It sounds as though
you helped him get that reputation."

Nett nodded at her father's side.

Scamman continued, "We wanted to thank you by
asking you to come to our farm in North Saco for
Christmas dinner. But the authorities say they have
confined you here, to keep the farm going and protect it
from any would-be marauders...and we understand that
Elmer Swan nearly guaranteed Curtis Cove's gaining a
long-run reputation as a center for smuggling....down
here in a remote corner of Biddeford. So...since you
cannot come to our home, we are going to bring
Christmas here. Nett's mother, brother and two sisters
will be coming with us. We will bring the food and some
gifts. All the two of you have to do is cut a Christmas tree
and keep on doing what you are already doing. Have
plenty of wood for hot fires. The ALMANAC says it's
going to be very cold. If we can get help with chores, we'll
bring bedding and sleep on the floor; and we expect you,
Dan, to sleep under the same roof with us...on the floor of
the kitchen."

Dan was overwhelmed. He couldn't believe his
own ears nor say anything. In fact, tears began to well up
in his eyes as he reached across a thousand years of social
space to shake hands with Mr. Scamman. Scamman, a
rather blunt and gruff, but kindly man, put out his hand
and smiled, "It's all right, Dan; it's all right. I cried, too,
when I found out that Nett was safe. And we went to

town as soon as we could to talk with the authorities. We came straight down from town."

They all ate a quick lunch, and Nett and Dan went to the barnyard to bid them good-bye.

"See you Christmas morning," Scamman remarked as he and his son drove the horse down the lane, bells jingling at the horse's neck.

As they disappeared into the Highway, Dan turned to Nett and said, "Your father, a good man; he cares for people."

Nett nodded and returned to the house. She could hardly believe her ears and father either. She mused, "He must love me more than he's ever said."

Chapter XIX

Christmasfest...

The day dawned clear and crisp over Bayberry Point. Dan awoke very early, both excited and apprehensive about what might happen. Even before Nett called him to breakfast, he decided to visit his little house to see if it was all right, then take the long walk to the beach at the head of Amanda's Cove and take a look at the day from his perch on Bayberry Point, then stroll along the shingled shore between there and the Curtis farm.

He frightened a couple of field mice in his house, saw that they had eaten into some crackers he'd left on the shelf, made a nest in the eastern wall. He also observed that the water he'd left in the pail had frozen, bending the pail slightly. So he took it out on the porch, banged it, and knocked the ice out. But it had not damaged the pail so he strolled down the hill to the well, hoping he could get a drink of water. It was quite frozen, but some water trickled from the side, so he knew that the spring in the bottom was still working. He couldn't dip the water to get a drink, but he did get down on his hands and knees put his mouth to the surface to take a sip. It tasted so good he took several swallows...only to look up to see a mother deer watching him. He froze in his crouching position so as not to frighten her and her offspring. Soon she edged out on the marsh, following the woods around to the west.

He then walked back up the hill, paying particular attention to Amanda's Tomb, a name he'd recently given the pile of rocks covering her dead body. He talked to her for several minutes, finally said, "Ah don' know what's gonna happen to you and me, but Merry Christmas anyway."

Practically in tears, he set off through the Thorn Path, named after he'd torn his arms carrying Amanda from the beach. The snow was fairly deep since the path hadn't been used recently. He observed rabbit crossings and some evidence that a male deer had followed it for a few feet before veering off toward the marsh. A few frozen red berries clung to the low bushes, and he picked one to suck. This puckered his face, it was so sour!

Coming out of the woods, he climbed the steep rock bank over which he had rolled Amanda's body those many months ago, looked out through the mouth of the cove to see the water seeming to steam. The east was a pale yellow, from the Biddeford Pool skies to those over Cape Porpoise. He likened it to an early summer apple. Screwing up his courage, he walked along that very same beach where his misery had begun in midsummer, picked up a stone and skipped it along the calm surface of the water, then at half tide. He did this several times, always enjoying the way the rock hugged the surface without sinking. He also noticed that the western sky was becoming clear blue so knew that the Scamman family would not run into foul weather coming or going from their farm.

On Bayberry Point he climbed to his perch and again noted the yellow sky, blue over the marsh and the mottled land between him and the Curtis house. It had many colors, white of the snow, green of the small evergreens, brown of the low bushes, with an occasional bright red dot...the remains of last summer's fruit.

Sensing that it might be getting late, he descended from his low perch and waded through the low brush between him and the tiny cove separating Bayberry and Curtis Points, again noting many rabbit tracks. Reaching the windrows of small smooth rocks along the shore, he found one that was pure white, picked it up, felt its velvety surface, put it in his pocket. He looked for its mates, found none, dropped down the beach to find a huge lobster stranded in a small pool. He was of two minds, one to rescue it and toss it into deep water and the other to take it to the house. The latter impulse prevailed, so he picked it up carefully so as not to get bitten and proceeded to the house...knowing Nett could cook it for them to eat or give it to her parents. He'd brought home lots of lobsters in the past so it was rather commonplace.

Finally reaching the barn with his prize catch, he dropped it into a bucket of seaweed and went immediately to his milking and feeding chores.

Shortly afterward, he heard Nett greeting her family in a high-pitched voice. She was obviously very happy. He didn't slack his working pace but soon heard her father's voice above all the rest, "Where's Dan?" Nett evidently pointed to the barn, for soon Mr. Scamman was entering the stables and greeting him.

"Merry Christmas, Dan!"

"Same to you, suh!" Dan exclaimed yet keeping his reserve.

"Glad to see you working, Dan," Scamman blurted, also feeling a bit uncomfortable in the presence of his black friend.

"Thank you, suh," Dan responded.

"When you finish, Dan, come in to breakfast, I want you to meet Nett's mother and younger sisters."

"Yes, suh," Dan agreed, his heart pounding since all of this was still so strange to him.

Not long afterward, Dan rapped on the kitchen door, then entered, still somewhat cautiously after all of his years of obedience training.

During the next six or eight hours Dan had the experience of his life, one that he could hardly believe for many days afterward. The Scamman family had also brought a larger tree than the one he and Nett could find. They all pitched in to decorate both trees with strung popcorn and cranberries. They even lit tiny candles to put on the ends of the branches, something Dan had never seen before in his entire life.

And food! There seemed to be no end of it. For breakfast, they had something that Nett's mother, Jeannette, called chicken pie with gravy, gravy and more gravy. And breakfast became dinner so quickly that Dan wasn't sure what meal he was eating. There was turkey that Mr. Scamman had raised himself, goose, too. And pies of every kind: three kinds of apple, mince, squash, pumpkin! Which to choose? So Dan accepted some of each when Jeannette offered him that choice. Also vegetables they could never raise at Curtis Farm.

Dan had heard of giving gifts in great number, but he had never experienced it. He was always lucky to get or give one or two. So he felt uneasy when the Scamman family, one by one, began giving him presents...a heavy

winter coat from Mr. and Mrs. Scamman, a harmonica
from Nett's younger sisters, a new axe from her brother,
and from Nett: a bright red sweater she had knit. He had
seen her working on it during the fall, but never once
thought who it might be for. Dan was in tears when he
said, "Thank you, thank you for everything. I'm sorry I
have nothing for you."

Jeannette spoke first. "You gave us our daughter by
saving her life. We are most grateful for that, Dan. No
gift could be more precious."

The others followed suit, and Nett, too, cried. Nor
could Dan keep the tears back. Then they all stood in a
circle, hand in hand, including Dan, to sing some of the
hymns they knew best. When they had finished, Dan
broke into his favorite spiritual, "Over Jordan," and they
eventually all joined him until the rafters seemed to echo
their joy.

For Dan another highlight of the day was the music
that Nett's brother and sisters played, they on violins and
he on his harmonica. It reminded him of the music of his
boyhood around the campfire on the plantation, and it
made him cry. But he looked around the Scamman
family's faces; and they, too, were crying. Again, he could
not believe that this was all happening to him.

After dinner Henry Scamman suggested that Dan
and they explore the area. They began in the barn cupola
by getting an overview. Then they visited Dan's little
house, Amanda's Tomb, the well, Amanda's Beach,
Bayberry Point Perch, Curtis Cove Beach, Timber Point
and Little River. The wind was brisk but the sun shone.
Dan enjoyed being able to talk about the area. Nett added
her own knowledge.

Getting back to the barn at midafternoon, Henry Scamman bruskly announced. "Gotta get back to do chores at the farm in North Saco, so we hafta leave soon to make it by early evening. Moon should help us by the time we get to town."

So the Scamman family gathered their things, went to the barn to harness their horse, and prepared to leave. Just before they got into the sleigh, Henry Scamman turned to Dan and Nett to say, "I have permission from the authorities to tell you that you are to stay here, let nobody in to talk with you. Next week there will be details on the Curtis trial. Ralph has been contacted and is on his way home. When he gets here, of course, he'll take over and things may be different and difficult. But I think that everything's gonna turn out all right."

Each member of the family stared at Mr. Scamman. He had waited until the day of joy was behind them before making this announcement. Jeannette hugged her daughter good-bye, then all shook hands with Dan. Mr. Scamman then turned to Dan to say, "Again, thank you for what you did. We'll never forget it. And when this whole nasty affair with Curtis is over, we want you to visit us at our farm in North Saco. Meanwhile, I am prepared to testify on your behalf when the case gets to court. Curtis was a prominent man in the two towns, but I think that he went too far this time. He will probably stay in jail a long, long time."

Nett turned to her father, hugged him as she had never hugged him before. He responded similarly. She then went to stand beside Dan and addressed her father, "We'll tend the farm and honor your wishes, dad."

Dan could see that Mr. Scamman was proud of his daughter.

The family climbed into the sleigh and were down the lane before anybody could get irritated by the hound's barking incessantly in his house by the cow stable.

Very matter of factly, Nett turned toward the kitchen and Dan toward the henyard to feed the chickens.

Chapter XX

Of Many Trials

Within a fortnight Ralph Curtis had returned to the farm. Since he was still rather sickly, he told Nett and Dan that they should go on with their work as they had done since the horrible night of the murder. He apologized for his father's behavior but told the two farmhands that he was not surprised that his father was in trouble. He had always feared for his step-mother. Dan and Nett felt badly for Ralph, told him so, and the three of them held many a winter night's discussion about their futures. Ralph was especially entertaining as he told the two about his life in the Army, how he had frozen at his gun when sighting the first Confederate soldier he was supposed to kill at Front Royal. He also regaled them with some of the stories other soldiers had told him about their experiences. And he was moved when he told of his days in Washington and his seeing President Lincoln...and how OLD he looked. Ralph endeared himself to both Nett and Dan because they saw him trying to help with the farm work as he limped about with his bad leg. Nett played nurse, too, not only aiding with all the housework but also bandaging Ralph's still weeping wounds.

During the second week of Ralph's homecoming, he and Dan got a summons from Counselor King, indicating that they must come to Biddeford. So Dan harnessed Red to the sleigh and they slogged to town through slushy roads filled with mud.

Dan was very nervous, told Ralph so, and Ralph calmly told him that whatever had happened had happened. It was not his fault.

"But what if they put me in jail for burying Amanda without telling anybody?" Dan asked, almost whining as he spoke.

"You had no other choice, Dan," Ralph assured him.

"But what about Elmer Swan? I knew he must have escaped from jail but I gave him a hiding place."

"Sure, you had a choice," Ralph said, almost chuckling, you could hide him or get a bullet in your head."

After this exchange in the sleigh, Dan rode quietly for minutes at a time listening intently to the harness rattling and the bells jingling. He also observed to Ralph that they were passing Cousin Amos's farm, and wondered aloud about Amos's caving barn roof. He also got even more nervous as they reached the edges of town.

Ralph said little. He was listening to his own counsel and wondering what would happen to his father whom he'd seen only once at Alfred prison   since returning.

At the counselor's office in Biddeford they learned that their appeal to move the trial from Alfred to Saco had been approved in order to make "easier use of local witnesses," also because they believed that Henry Scamman was an important enough man to carry weight on Dan's behalf. Dan wasn't sure how he should react, but he smiled a lot during the discussions and returned directly to the farm even as Ralph got a friend to take him to Alfred to talk again with his father.

****

John Curtis's trial was held in Saco in early April. Fortunately, it was an early spring. The mayflowers were out in scented profusion. The woods were carpeted with dog-tooth violets. Mud season was over. A huge forest and grass fire in the Sanford-Waterboro area had filled the air with pungent smells of spring. Even Main streets in the two towns were reasonably uncluttered; the snowpiles in the alleys were melted. But both cities were buzzing with rumors, little knots of conversationalists and gossips, bold headlines in extra sheets in the papers which usually downplayed local news and relegated it to the inside pages. It was one of those situations where a prominent man had been found out and all of the lurid details were alive on many tongues. The moral of the case had been mentioned from every church pulpit, an example to be avoided like hellfire and damnation...even before any convictions had been handed down. And, of course, the fact of Nett's and Dan's living together on the farm came in for its share of attention, rumor, speculation, condemnation. Hence, when the trial began there was little neutrality among the populace. Yet, it was not too difficult to choose a jury to sit. After all, if one were not neutral about the possible facts and outcome, a jury seat was one of the best in the house, which predictably enough was full...that house being the new town hall built less than seven years before and one of the largest public arenas in the two communities.

Too, the streets were full of vendors and hawkers selling all kinds of sweets, nuts and the last fruits of winter's cellars. And it was hard to move along Main Street in Saco, from the railroad bridge at Cataract Falls to the Congregational Church at Main and Beach, there were so many wagons "down from the country." In fact Henry Scamman announced, "All North Saco is here."

Naturally enough, they knew him and his family, and the taste of scandal brought out many a dry mouth wanting stimulation. A few soldiers' uniforms mixed with the lighter colors of spring since the wounded and those on furlough joined to share the excitement.

****

The court case itself, while trying for Nett, Ralph and Dan, actually divulged little new information. It was noised about that Curtis's lawyer, Roy Shields, had attempted to get his client to plead "Guilty" and hence avoid public spectacle and scandal. But Curtis was clearly too proud a man to do that, stating on the stand that he had to do what he did...but was never clear as to why...something the prosecuting attorney pointed out several times to the jury.

Dan took the stand very nervously. He was certainly not used to looking out onto a sea of white faces, some of whom seemed very hostile. But just before he walked to the stand, Nett barely touched his arm and reassured him, "It's going to be all right, Dan."

Ralph, too, squeezed his hand. Shields, of course, saw and seized upon both gestures and treated them with innuendo. But the gestures comforted Dan.

Actually, the prosecuting attorney, Ray Lane, was quite gentle, simply getting Dan to say "Yes" or "No" to what seemed like a thousand questions pertaining to the story, step by step, from Amanda's first disappearance to the moment when Dan clubbed Curtis to get him off Nett when he tried to rape her in the barn.

Ralph watched his father's face carefully, saw it turn ashen gray, but never reflect remorse...even though his father had told him at the prison that he was sorry.

Curtis's attorney rattled Dan only once during the cross examination. After reviewing the facts related to Curtis's behavior the night he killed Mom Curtis, Attorney Shields pulled a question out of the blue.

"How did you know Amanda was dead when you buried her?"

Dan stared at Shields in disbelief, hesitated for a long time as he reviewed the burial scene in his own mind.

Shields stood over Dan waiting as though to pounce upon him, then for dramatic effect stressed Dan's silence to push him, "Come, Dan! You heard the question! Answer it!"

Dan's silence continued and again Shields pounced, "Dan! I asked you a question, 'How did you KNOW Amanda was dead?'"

Finally Dan spoke, "She had been in the ocean for three days. When I lifted her arm, it fell. My mammy teach me to listen to heart. She had no beat. Her body cold. She dead."

"She dead," Shields mocked.

"She dead, suh; I live with her two , three days, dead."

At that point Shields, posturing before the jury and playing to the audience in the hall, snarled with sarcasm, "You expect US to believe YOU, a BLACK man, believe Amanda was DEAD, when you haven't a shred of evidence to prove it?"

"Your honor," Prosecutor Lane shouted, "I object! Lawyer Shields's argument is *ad hominem* !"

The audience rumbled over the incident.

"Order in the courtroom!" the judge screamed, pounding his gavel.

Shields paused for effect, exclaimed, "Then, your honor, we'd best exhume the body!"

"Continue," said the judge, "you lost your petition to do that during our pre-trial hearings."

Shields tried another tack, posturing again before the jury. "Here we have no evidence to prove that Amanda was dead. We know that a BLACK man lived under the same roof..."

Lane was on his feet, "Your honor, the effort my worthy opponent is making to use Dan's blackness to impugn his integrity is unworthy of him, you or this court. I ask that he be asked to desist."

Dan breathed a sigh of relief even though he did
not fully understand all of this legal maneuvering. He
could tell from the tone of the lawyers' voices that Lane
was getting the better of the argument. Meanwhile, the
courtroom was boiling with citizen undercurrent and
unrest.

Again, the judge banged his gavel and warned the
observers to desist or the courtroom would be cleared.
Waiting for calm in the hall, he looked at Shields and
warned, "Either you stick to the facts of the case or step
down. Witness Henry Scamman as well as evidence from
Doctors Watts and Lord have cleared the integrity of Dan's
word and color. Proceed."

Shields gestured as though to continue; then
feeling he'd scored points with the jury, he gave them a
knowing look and turned the witness back to Lane.

Lane used the opportunity to speak to the jury,
speaking slowly and very deliberately. "Ladies and
gentlemen, the facts of this case are clear. John Curtis has
virtually admitted killing two women and nearly raping a
third. Dan's part in all this has been verified by the
sheriffs and coroner. Faced with similar pressures any of
us might have feared Curtis and be frightened into
burying Amanda as he did. He harbored a prison escapee
at the point of a gun. Any of us would have done
likewise. We know from testimony by Messrs Watts and
Lord that Dan's color does not deprive him of emotions
such as any of us might express, of love for Amanda, fear
of Curtis's strength and authority, anger at seeing another
human and animals being beaten. We must also
remember that in many respects Dan is in a foreign land.
Maine is not Virginia. Black society is not Yankee society.
And while he came as a slave, he is now a free man,
thanks to President Lincoln's Proclamation."

Then, turning to the judge, he concluded, "Your
honor, I think that this court will honor itself, the State of
Maine, and God if Mr. Curtis is declared guilty and Dan is

permitted to live out his life as a free man. He has earned that right."

Shields chose not to sum up except by innuendo, hoping again that he could count on local prejudice to save his client. At the close of his statement he looked at Curtis to say, "This man deserves to go free because he's been an upstanding member of his community. Need one be more, especially when he tried to save two black people from slavery?"

The jury was out for only a half hour during which time Dan, Nett and Ralph were closeted with Attorney Lane. They could hear the populace in the auditorium grumbling and rumbling with an occasional high-pitched voice expressing outrage at Shields. Together they comforted one another. Lane was especially helpful in explaining to Dan what had happened, expressing the belief that Shields had hurt Curtis's cause more than helping it. Dan thanked Lane for his support, especially for preventing them from forcing him to dig up Amanda. It was a warm spring day, sun pouring through the winter-battered windows, turning dust flecks into long light rays almost tangible enough to touch. The court clerk provided them with lots of lemonade for their thirst.

Soon the clerk called them back to the courtroom to hear the verdict. The citizen mumbling gradually quieted down after the judge banged his gavel, and all could have heard a pin drop.

The judge nodded to the jury foreman who slowly got to his feet to say, "Our judgment: murder in the first degree on both counts."

Again, the auditorium was abuzz.

Again, the judge banged his gavel.

The judge started to thank the jury, but he and the citizens gasped to see the foreman rise to say, "Your honor, we want to add a word to the verdict. We want to thank the Scamman family and Dan for what they have done for our town and we want to give a special welcome to Dan as a free man under President Lincoln's Proclamation."

The citizens applauded spontaneously and rose to their feet as a single person, only one or two clinging to their chairs and looking around to see what was happening..

For a moment the judge seemed taken back, but nodded approval as the foreman sat down, remarking, "You have taken the words from my mouth. I too, welcome Dan. And I want to say that this court and you good people of York County have honored our community, the State of Maine, our country and God on this day. Also, it's a victory for truth!"

Looking at Curtis, he announced, "I shall pass sentence at 10 A.M. on May 1st, court dismissed."

Again Pandemonium broke out in the auditorium, and Dan and his party were surrounded by people, some shaking hands with Lane, some with Ralph, and some with Dan. Doctors Lord and Watts waded through the crowd to say something special to Dan. Dan hardly knew how to respond but did the best he could do to smile through the tears rolling down his cheeks. A few women came forward to hug Nett. Some told Ralph they were sorry about his father and hoped he would come to town to see them.

When the crowd had partly dispersed, Dan looked across the courtroom to see officers escorting Curtis through a side door. He could not help but feel a twinge of sorrow for the tall man. After all, Curtis had harbored Amanda and him when they were in deep trouble and fleeing slavery. Ralph saw Dan staring at his father, turned and took Dan by the arm, saying quietly, "Come on, Dan, let's go home. The cows need milking; we can't let Smith do it another day. Maybe he's got the horses drunk!"

Turning to Nett, he said, "Have a good visit with your family. You're welcome back at the farm whenever you wish to return. He turned, stopped for a moment, caught his father's eyes just as Curtis looked back, then hid his own behind his hand.

Epilogue

Back on the farm Ralph and Dan fell back into routine, did the ploughing, cared for the animals, took time to watch the geese flying north in wavery V's and worked on a carpentry project for which Dan would always be grateful. They added a room to the barn, on the cove side, fixed it up for Dan, complete with a separate entrance, furnished it with the best of beds, chairs, and other accommodations. Ralph, too, saw that Dan got a whole new wardrobe, one appropriate for a newly freed man. Dan would never forget that visit to Saco where he not only bought clothes, with Ralph, who also needed to replace his army clothing with civilian togs, but he also visited Messrs Watts and Lord and took time to exchange tales with Wilbur Francis at the Saco House stable. And, of course, for most of the people in Saco he continued to be both a celebrity and a strange phenomenon. People he had never remembered seeing walked up to shake his hand...or simply stare.

Nett returned to the farm just before John Curtis was sentenced to life imprisonment. She continued to nurse Ralph back to health and comfort him for the loss of his father. So many times she said, "I'm sorry that I was partially at fault for what happened."

And so many times he responded, "You certainly can't be responsible for my father's lust and violence."

Throughout that summer Nett, Ralph and Dan ate most of their meals together, many on the porch where they could look out to sea or across to the mouth of

Amanda's Cove. Ralph and Nett got Dan to talk at length about Amanda.

Ralph spoke frankly to Dan, indicating that he was free to leave, to live in town, to take another job where he could improve himself more quickly, or whatever. This brought Dan close to devastation, but he told Ralph that he felt that this was his home and would like to stay. While Dan might seem to be a second class citizen, he came to appreciate his independence. Yet, he never forgot Amanda, learned from Nett how he could honor Amanda and his memory the more by laying flowers on her grave during the summer, weave wreathes from evergreen to lay on her tomb in the dead of winter.

Dan could see it coming, too. It began when he went to breakfast one morning and saw that Ralph had his arm around Nett...just after dawn. Somehow he felt that they had been up all night, for he had left them early in the evening watching the moon come up over Bayberry Point. He was discrete in saying, "Good morning," but he noticed that Ralph did not remove his arm from Nett's shoulder. He was glad, for he loved them both. Not long afterward they announced to him that they would soon be married. Dan was to tend the farm while they took a week to do it. For the first time in his life he embraced them both.

Together they continued to work shoulder to shoulder to improve and farm the rugged land, can vegetables and fruit, love the animals and respect their neighbors. Old Rex, the hound, died late that fall, and they immediately replaced him with a beautiful shepherd who was not only a good watch dog but very playful with all of them.

In due time Nett became pregnant, delivered a baby
boy in mid-November as the first snowflakes drifted
across the point.   That child was followed by identical
male twins, born in May and finally her first girl, born on
Christmas Day and named Amanda.   Dan loved them all,
nurtured them while their parents were away, came to be
regarded by the children as "Uncle Dan."   He told them
story after story, about his boyhood and the South; but he
became so masterful at telling Maine stories that he was
even in demand in town.   Sometimes he felt that he was
more of a freak than he liked; but he enjoyed so much
hearing people laugh that he put his feelings aside.   So he
kept his base at the farm while becoming somewhat of a
celebrity between Portland and Portsmouth.

The boys grew up to be farmers, one of them a
farmer of the sea, a lobsterman who tended his traps, dug
clams in Little River and delivered fish to Biddeford and
Saco deep into the twentieth century. Amanda moved to
Saco during her high school years to attend the newly
opened Thornton Academy, met a Bowdoin man who
would become a doctor and practice in Portland.   They
were a close family, never failing to hold reunions at
Christmas and the Fourth of July.   And they never failed
to remember Dan with small gifts.   The year Amanda
graduated from Thornton they held a huge party, inviting
people from miles around.   The Scamman and Curtis
families joined at many a picnic, either in North Saco
along the banks of the Saco River or at Fortunes Rocks
where their huge clam chowders became famous
throughout York County and among the out-of-town
strangers who had begun to build cottages along the beach
on Amanda's Cove and Long Beach stretching to
Biddeford Pool..

Dan had but two regrets. He hated to see the new cottages crowding space which he regarded almost his own, space which had allowed him to enjoy the geese, the ever-changing sky, the many colors of the marsh, the space made holy by Amanda's remembered presence. Also he regretted that Amanda could not have lived to savor some of his joys. And sometimes when he visited her grave he told her what was happening and seemed to hear her voice answering him through the wind...

Dan, too, lived into his eighties, dying in the great flu epidemic of World War I. Ralph and Nett buried him under the rock pile beside Amanda.

The foundation of Dan's and Amanda's little house has long since caved in. Ashes from the fire that burned it down have long since vanished into the earth. Only a hollow remains. The oaks tower into the sea and sunset-washed skies over the marsh. Birds have sewn blueberry and fern seeds in that basement hollow.

But close beside the site of the house the rockpile stands, a monument to Dan's sweat, loyalty and love. Skunks, raccoons and squirrels scoot and skitter over the stones, then pass into the underbrush. Deer, possibly offspring from those Amanda and Dan watched and treasured, still traverse the marsh at dawn and dusk, sometimes coming to that self-same wellspring from which Dan and Amanda drank.

Now that spring rises and nurtures the lawn of a
large grey house, described by a local poet as

    Clay blue graydeep in lacey greens
    perching high over heather
    purple turning brown
    in frosty weather
    marsh olive colors
    becoming fawn
    while
    two deer
    at dawn
    chasing full moon
    down the west
    their dancing shadows
    leaping east
    as honking geese
    in mysterious ways...
    egrets wading gingerly
    in shallow pools
    to fool a minnow:
        Ah, PLUCK
           breakfast luck!
sun,
        no Peeping Tom, but
        rising over oakly trees
        just in time
        to see the breeze...

This house and two others grace the hill where
Amanda and Dan had their life and being. Joining the
stars and moon and barn owls each night are lights from

several houses, sometimes turning deep murky nights into a Christmas-like atmosphere. Heavy leaf growth a-summers provides shade like that which the black couple enjoyed. And a-winters, today's residents can see all the way to Amanda's Cove as well as to the cupola on the old Curtis barn. Other lights suggest that "civilization" may have arrived.

But sometimes when a far-off whippoorwill whips or a hound, owl or coyote howls, it is said that two ghosts float through the oaks, dancing as they did in life, signs of love and joy in a world all too filled with hate and fear. And on those eerie nights, the wind seems to whisper, "Amanda, Amanda, Amanda..."